小王子

Le Petit Prince

中英雙語典藏版

安東尼·聖修伯里——著、繪

姚文雀——譯 曾銘祥——繪

收錄

〈作家生平解析〉

晨星出版

導讀

所有的大人都會是孩子

吳淡如

　　小王子是一本童話，也可以不是一本童話；是一個寓言，也可以不是一個寓言。但如果你不是圖書館的圖書分類人員，不必因此傷腦筋。

　　它是什麼都不重要，如果你要為它的屬性爭辯得面紅耳赤的話，你就落入了聖修伯里的「寓言」之中，變成只關心重要事情的「商人」，「重要的事情」在小王子的字典裡是有點諷刺的，比如：

　　假如你跟大人們說：「我看到一棟玫瑰色磚塊砌成的漂亮房子，窗戶上綴滿了天竺葵，鴿子們都棲息在屋頂上。」他們絕對對那棟房子沒有任何想法。你必須說：「我看見一棟價值十億的房子。」他們就會大叫：「那一定是一棟很漂亮的房子！」

　　我想聖修伯里一直是個孩子，在他心裡，在法國人眼裡，在全世界看小王子的人的靈魂裡，他就是那個小王子。不肯長大，永遠不會長大。他在四十四歲那年的七月三十一日早晨，駕著飛機離開科西嘉島，從此不見蹤影，五十年來所有小王子的讀者，無不在悲傷之餘發揮想像力，認為他跟小王子一樣，你永遠找不到他的屍體，他會回到他的星星上，在夜晚，你仰頭看星空，會看到五億小鈴鐺，他就在其中的一顆星上，因為有他，所有的星星都變得有意義……

　　所以幾年前，證實在科西嘉島附近海域找到他失事的飛機殘骸，沒有人認為這是「好消息」。他會每天把花兒放在玻璃罩下，並小心翼翼守護著他的小綿羊，不是嗎？

　　小王子在全世界擁有可怕的讀者群，不過聖修伯里一定希望我們不要太關心，否則我們會變成只對數目有興趣的，第四個星球上面的商人。

讓我們來關心眞實的故事本身。

小王子是一個很好看的故事，很動人的故事，很適合孩子看的故事（不管是現實的孩子或心靈的孩子），也很適合大多數已經變得有點無趣的大人。

當你看一本書的時候，你可以變成一個再創造者，這就是一本好書了。不分教育程度、職業、年齡、性別、國籍和人種都可以會心微笑，都能用自己的方法去讀它，那更是一本動人的超級好書。小王子是這樣的一本書。

這樣的讚美，我並不覺得肉麻，它確實爲我打開一扇非常壯觀的窗戶。第一次讀小王子時，我十二歲，正處於懷疑自己完全不被世界了解的年齡，我的國中一年級國文老師送我小王子，讓我發現生命的一個出口。故事啊！多麼美妙的天籟。在我心中，做一個說故事的人，變成一種神聖的職業。我也不再懷疑，爲什麼「大人」們不了解我呢？爲什麼大人們了解事情的方式，和觀看世界的角度，和我完全不一樣呢？我依然質疑，但我可以想像自己在地球旅行，不時和小王子交換一個知己的微笑。那時的小王子，對我來說是一個志同道合的朋友。

後來我變成了一個「大人」，長大了的人。我忽然發現自己又從小王子中讀到了新的東西。看哪，我旁邊的世界，充滿其他「大人」——再也不心懷天眞，不可愛的人——竟然像小王子造訪過的小行星上的人一樣！

有穿著貂皮，孤獨坐在自己星球上的國王，只想「理性」地下命令控制一切；有些人（其實我們都是）像「驕傲自大的人」，只愛被崇拜，除了讚美什麼也聽不見；有些人像酒鬼，自暴自棄只爲了想忘記自己的自暴自棄；有些人像「商人」，只爲數字忙個半死，想占有再占有，其實對他們的占有物非常無助；有些人遵守「規則」如同點燈夫，不知自己爲誰而忙，爲何而忙；有些人是寫大部頭書的地理學家，只關心死的東西，對有生命的一切一點也不感興趣。長大了，小王子是我憤世嫉俗的朋友。

後來，我又在小王子中讀到生命的矛盾律。

國王說，我相信我的星球有一隻愛叫的老老鼠，我偶爾判牠的死刑，那麼牠的生殺大權就操在你手裡，但每一回你都得饒牠，因爲牠是我們僅有的犯人。

　　驕傲自大的人說，崇拜的意思，就是你認爲我是這個星球上最帥、穿得最漂亮、最有錢、而且最聰明的人；雖然，星球上只有他一個人⋯⋯

　　面對酒鬼，「爲什麼喝酒？」小王子追問。「爲了遺忘！」酒鬼說。「遺忘什麼？」「爲了遺忘我很可恥。」「爲什麼可恥？」「因爲我喝酒！」

　　大人總是矛盾的。小王子也是矛盾的。他愛他的玫瑰花卻又不知怎麼愛她，他離開她但又想念她；玫瑰花也是矛盾的，她愛他、依靠他，卻折磨他；狐狸是矛盾的，牠要小王子馴養牠，但又在他離開時捨不得他⋯⋯

　　愛總是矛盾的，聖修伯里的矛盾是所有人的矛盾。

　　這時，小王子是一個有同情心的天使。

　　後來，當我的弟弟離開這個世界，感到無助時我會翻開小王子，讀到「你知道⋯⋯太遠了。我不能帶著這個身體走，太重了⋯⋯」，我也把自己交給悲傷，每一個像鈴鐺般的星星，也都化成了淚水。我只能祈禱著，小王子在其他的星球，有更可愛的旅程⋯⋯像聖修伯里所堅信的，離開是一個旅程的新開始，是一種出發，是另一個飛翔的開始。

　　所以，如果，如果你有一天到沙漠旅行，請不要匆匆趕路，如果有個金黃色頭髮的小人兒出現，他愛笑，又不肯回答問題，你就知道他是誰了。萬一有這種事，請安慰安慰我吧。捎個口信告訴我，他回來了。

　　你知道嗎？我不想做個「大人」，因爲我一直不肯在心裡忘記⋯⋯小王子。

　　小王子這樣的結束，我的嚕嗦，也這樣的結束罷。

前言

希望所有讀到這本書的小孩都能原諒我，首先我將這本書獻給一位大人。

我有相當充足的理由：這個大人是我在這世界上最要好的朋友。

還有另一個理由：這位大人瞭解每件事，即使是有關小孩的書也一樣。

以及第三個理由：這個大人住在法國，他在飢餓寒冷之際需要一些鼓勵。

如果我所說的這些理由都還不夠好的話，請不要介意我把這本書獻給曾經是小孩的他。

所有的大人都曾經是小孩，雖然，只有少數的人記得這件事。

因此，我將我的獻詞更改為：

獻給 里昂‧維德──當還是小男孩的他

聖修伯里 寫於美國

第 1 章

　　我六歲的時候，在一本書上看到一張很有趣的插畫，那本書叫做《大自然的真實故事》，內容是描述關於原始雨林的故事。那張插圖畫的是一隻蟒蛇正在吞食獵物的模樣。你看，就是下面這張圖。

書上寫：「蟒蛇連嚼都不嚼，把獵物整個吞下去以後，就一動也不動，直到牠們經過六個月的長眠，消化完所有吃下的食物。」

於是我開始想像我的叢林冒險，並且用一支彩色鉛筆成功完成我人生的第一幅畫作。我的一號作品，就像下面的這張圖：

我把這幅傑作拿給大人們看時，還問他們有沒有被這張圖嚇到。

他們卻說：「嚇到？為什麼會被帽子嚇到？」

我畫的根本不是帽子。明明是一隻蟒蛇正在消化牠吃進去的大象！於是我又畫了一張蟒蛇內部的透視圖，我想大人們應該就能看懂了。唉，大人總是需要清楚的解釋。

我的二號作品畫成像下一頁那樣。

　　大人們這次看完的反應是叫我把這些蟒蛇圖，不管是外觀或透視的圖都丟掉，只要好好地學習地理、歷史、算術和文法就好。於是，我六歲那年，就放棄成為畫家這個有趣的職業。我對一號作品和二號作品的失敗，感到十分沮喪，大人從來都不靠自己去了解一些事情；而小孩老是要解釋給他們聽，真的好煩。

　　因此，我只好選擇另一個職業：學習開飛機。現在，我幾乎飛過全世界的國家，而以前唸的地理也真的很有用，我一眼就可分辨出中國和美國亞歷桑納州的不同。這對在夜晚迷航的人來說，是個很可貴的經驗。

　　在這職業生涯裡，我跟很多嚴肅的人打交道過，花許多時間跟各種大人接觸，也曾經很仔細地觀察他們，但我對他們的印象並沒有多大的改變。

　　每當我遇到一個看起來似乎滿聰明的人，我就會給他看我一直保存著的一號作品，這樣我就能知道對方是否是個有理解力的人。然而這些大人都說:「這是一頂帽子。」於是,我就不會再跟他解釋什麼蟒蛇、原始雨林,或星星了。我會遷就他們,談談橋牌、高爾夫球、政治,還有領帶等等的話題。這樣一來,這些大人就會非常高興他們遇到一個無所不談的人。

第 2 章

　　就這樣，我一個人孤獨地活著，因為找不到真正可以談心的人。然而六年前，我在撒哈拉沙漠發生的飛航意外，改變了一切。那次，我的飛機引擎出了點毛病，當時既沒有維修技師在旁邊，也沒有半個路人經過，我只好自己扛下這高難度的修復大任。這可是生死關頭：我的飲用水存量是撐不過八天的。

　　我在那裡的第一個晚上，想到要睡在方圓千里之內都渺無人跡的地方，就覺得自己比一個因為船難，在海中攀著浮木漂流的水手，還要孤立無援。

　　所以，你可以想像得到，第二天早上，當我被奇怪又微弱的聲音吵醒時，我有多驚訝了。那個聲音說：

　　「拜託——幫我畫一隻綿羊。」

　　「什麼！」

　　「幫我畫一隻綿羊。」

　　我像被雷電擊中般跳了起來。我揉揉眼睛，看到一個十分奇特的小人，他正睜大眼睛看著我。這裡有一張他的肖像，是我後來盡最大努力畫出來的。不過，他本人比這張畫更好看。畢竟，沒能將他傳神地畫下來並不是我的錯！我的繪畫能力早在我六歲時，就被那些大人們毀了，我除了大蟒蛇的外觀和透視圖，再也沒畫過別的東西。

　　我目瞪口呆地站著，看著這個如幻影般突然出現的人。別忘了，我現在迫降在這個方圓千里渺無人跡的沙漠。而眼前這個小人兒既不像是在沙漠裡迷路；也不像疲憊、飢餓、口渴或害怕的人，況且從他的身上一點兒都看不出他正迷失在這個沙漠。當我終於回過神說得出話來時，我問他：「你在這兒做什麼？」

　　他卻緩緩地重複著他所說的話，彷彿在說一件很重要的事，「拜託──幫我畫一隻綿羊……」

　　當一個人被某種神祕力量震懾住時，是絕對不敢不服從的。在四下罕無人跡，又面臨死亡威脅的情況下，我從口袋裡掏出一張紙和一枝筆，卻忽然想到我只學過地理、歷史、算術和文法這些科目，我有些彆扭地，告訴這個小傢伙我不知道該怎麼畫。

　　他回答說：「沒關係，幫我畫一隻綿羊……」

　　可是我從沒畫過綿羊！於是，我就畫了一張以前畫過的蟒蛇外觀圖給他。接下來這小傢伙說的話卻讓我大吃一驚。

　　「不是，不是，我不要蟒蛇把大象吃進去的圖。蟒蛇是一種危險的生物，大象又太大了。我是從很小的地方來的，那裡每樣東西都很小。我要的是一隻綿羊，幫我畫一隻綿羊……」

我只好再畫一張。他仔細地看了我的畫，然後說：「不行，這隻羊已經病得太嚴重了。再幫我畫一隻。」

於是我又畫了一張。

這次，他溫和且靦腆地笑。「你自己看，」他說，「畫上的動物不是綿羊。這是一隻公羊。牠頭上有角！」

於是我再重畫。但是這張也和先前那幾張的命運一樣，被拒絕了。

「這隻太老了！我要能活久一點，健康的小綿羊。」

我開始感到厭煩，一心只想快點修理飛機的引擎。我隨便畫了這張圖，丟下一句話：

「這是裝羊的盒子，你要的那隻羊在盒子裡面。」

沒想到，我的小評審臉上流露出欣喜的光芒：

「這就是我想要的！你覺得這隻羊需不需要餵牠吃很多草呢？」

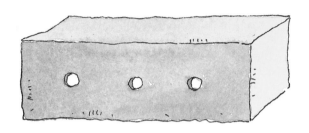

「什麼意思？」

「因為我住的地方，每樣東西都很小⋯⋯」

「盒子裡已經有足夠的草，」我說：「我幫你畫了隻非常小的綿羊。」

他把頭湊近紙邊看畫：「沒那麼小──你看！⋯⋯牠睡著了⋯⋯」

這就是我遇見小王子的經過。

第 3 章

　　我花了很長一段時間，才知道他是從哪兒來的。小王子總是問我一大堆問題，但他對於我的提問卻好像聽不見似的，我只能從他偶然提及的事，一點一滴地拼湊出真相。

　　比如當他第一次看到我的飛機時，他問我：「那是什麼東西？」

　　「那不是『東西』。它會飛喔，那是飛機，是『我的』飛機。」

　　我很驕傲地告訴他，我可是一個飛行員。沒想到他馬上大叫：「什麼！你是從天上掉下來的？」

　　「是啊。」我謙虛地回答。

　　「哇！真好玩！」小王子爆發出一連串笑聲，這使我有些火大。我希望他能以嚴肅的態度，來看待我的不幸。然而，他接著說：「那你也是從天上來的囉?!你來自哪一個星球？」

　　這時，一個奇妙的想法也許能解釋他的存在，我接著問他：「你是來自另一個星球？」

他沒有回答，只是盯著我的飛機，輕輕地搖頭：「顯然你搭的東西，不可能來自太遠的地方，對吧？」然後他就沉浸在自己的世界中。過了好一會兒，他從口袋裡掏出我畫的綿羊，像寶貝般仔細地看了一遍。

　　你可以想像得到，我對「另一個星球」這一知半解的訊息有多麼好奇，我想找到更多線索。

　　「小人兒，你是從哪裡來的？你住在哪裡？你要把我的羊帶去哪裡？」

　　他沉思了一會兒，然後回答：「你畫給我的盒子是最棒的，即使是晚上，我的羊也能舒服地住在裡面。」

　　「當然囉！如果你人很不錯的話，我還可以幫你畫一條繩子，這樣白天你就可以把羊拴起來。喔，對了！還要一根柱子才行。」

　　小王子被這個想法嚇了一跳：「把牠拴起來？好奇怪的想法！」

　　「如果你不拴住牠，牠就會好奇地到處亂逛，然後就會走丟了。」

　　這個小人兒又笑了起來：「你覺得牠可以跑去哪兒？」

　　「哪裡都有可能啊。牠會一直向前跑。」

　　沒想到小王子憂鬱地說：「沒關係。我住的地方每樣東西都好小！」接著，他的語氣透露一絲哀傷，「即使往前走，也走不了多遠……」

第 4 章

　　於是我有了第二個重大發現：小王子居住的星球，和一棟房子差不多大！

　　我一點也不驚訝。我知道，除了地球、木星、火星、金星等已經被命名的行星，還有數以百計的星球存在，有些星球甚至小到用望遠鏡都很難看見。當天文學家發現這種小行星時，就會幫它編個號碼，當做它的名字。舉例來說，他可以把他發現的星球叫做「小行星 325 號」。

　　我有很充分的理由相信：小王子是來自小行星 B612。這顆小行星只在西元一九〇九年，被一位土耳其的天文學家透過望遠鏡看過一次。

　　當時，這位天文學家在發現這個星球後，在「國際天文學會議」上提出論點，但沒有人相信他，因為他穿的是土耳其的傳統服裝。大人們，就是這個樣子……

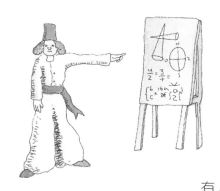

不過值得慶幸的是，為了小行星 B612 的聲譽，土耳其的統治者下令民眾都要改穿歐式服裝，違抗命令者就是死罪！當西元一九二〇年這位天文學家穿著光鮮亮麗的西裝，再一次發表演說，這次所有人都相信他了。

我之所以如此詳細地說明小行星的事，包括它的編號，完全是為了大人們。大人們喜歡數字。當你提到你交到新朋友時，他們從不會想知道那些真正重要的事情，他們絕不會問：「他的聲音好不好聽？他最喜歡什麼遊戲？他有沒有收集蝴蝶標本的習慣？」通常他們只會問：「他幾歲？他有幾個兄弟姊妹？他體重多重？他爸爸賺多少錢？」

大人們總是覺得，只有這些數字才能夠幫助他們了解一個人。

假如你跟大人們說：「我看到一棟玫瑰色磚塊砌成的漂亮房子，窗戶上綴滿了天竺葵，鴿子們都棲息在屋頂上。」他們絕對對那棟房子沒有任何想法。你必須說：「我看見一棟價值十億的房子。」他們就會大叫：「那一定是一棟很漂亮的房子！」

所以如果你對他們說：「小王子存在的證據是：他很討人喜歡、他很愛笑，而且他想要一隻羊。如果有人想要一隻羊，就可以證明他的存在。」他們只會聳聳肩，覺得你像個小孩一樣。但是如果你跟他們說：「他來自小行星 B612。」他們就會相信，並且不會再用一些雜七雜八的問題煩你。

大人們就是這樣。你不可以跟他們作對，小孩子需要非常容忍大人們。

當然囉，我們這些很懂生命意義的人對數字根本不屑一顧。我想用童話故事的方式，開始敘述這個故事。我會這樣說：「很久很久以前，有一個小王子，住在一個沒比他自己大多少的小行星上；而且，他需要一個朋友……」

對於那些很懂生命意義的人來說，這個故事可以因此顯得更真實。

我不希望這本書變得無足輕重。對我來說，回憶這些事十分的痛苦。自從我的朋友小王子帶著他的羊離開，已經過了六年，我在這裡寫下他的故事，是因為我永遠不會忘記他。忘記朋友是一件令人感傷的事，不是每個人都能有交心的朋友。況且如果我忘記他了，我可能就會變得跟那些除了數字之外，對什麼事都不感興趣的大人一樣……

由於這些想法，我買了幾枝鉛筆和一盒顏料。以我現在的年紀，很難重新學習畫圖 —— 尤其自從六歲那年畫過大蟒蛇的外觀和透視圖以後。但我還是會盡可能地畫得很像,但我不太確定成果是好是壞。也許有一張畫得還不錯,也許另一張就不行。而關於小王子的身高,我也犯了些錯誤,有的畫得太高,有的又畫得太矮;我也不太確定他衣服的顏色,只能憑記憶儘量東拼西湊畫出原貌。我可能會在某些重要的細節上出錯,但你必須原諒我,因為我的朋友從來不對我解釋任何事,也許他以為我像他一樣,只可惜……我根本「不能」經由盒子透視裡面的羊。大概是因為變老了,我有點像那些大人了。

第 5 章

　　我每天會透過我們的談話，來認識小王子居住的星球，以及他的離開、他的旅程。因此，第三天，我聽到關於猴麵包樹的危險性。

　　這次我得感謝綿羊的話題，因為小王子突然被這個問題困住，很擔心地問我：

　　「綿羊真的會吃灌木叢，對不對？」

　　「對啊！」

　　「喔！那太好了！」

　　我不明瞭為什麼綿羊會吃灌木叢的事很重要，但是，小王子接著說：

　　「那麼牠們也吃猴麵包樹囉？」

　　我跟小王子說，猴麵包樹和灌木叢一點都不像，那是像教堂般高大的樹；而且，就算他帶著一群大象，這些大象連一棵猴麵包樹也沒辦法啃完。

　　一群大象這個想法讓小王子笑了。「那我們必須把一隻隻大象疊起來……」接著他又說，「但猴麵包樹長成大樹之前，也是一棵小樹呀！」

「那倒是真的。不過為什麼要讓你的羊去吃猴麵包樹的幼苗呢？」

　　他說：「噢，這還要解釋啊？」他的口氣彷彿這是一個很簡單的問題，我卻必須聽到解釋才能理解。

　　原來小王子居住的星球就跟其他星球一樣，長著有益的植物和有害的植物，所以也有好種子跟壞種子。然而種子是看不到的，因為它們都很神祕地沉睡在地底，直到其中一顆想甦醒。剛開始時，這顆小種子會羞怯地伸伸懶腰，然後向著太陽長出嫩芽。如果長出來的是蘿蔔或玫瑰的嫩芽，就可以讓它們自由發展；如果是有害植物的芽，你就必須在辨認出來的當下，立刻把它拔除。

　　而小王子的星球上就有一些可怕的植物種子——那就是猴麵包樹的種子。它們遍布於星球各地的土壤裡，一旦它們占有地盤，就不可能把它們除掉，猴麵包樹會將根鑽入泥土，接管整個星球。更別說如果星球太小而猴麵包樹太多的話，那些樹就會把星球擠爆……

　　「這是自律的問題，」小王子後來告訴我，「早上盥洗後，我必須很小心地為我的星球做晨間的清理：拔掉猴麵包樹的嫩芽。因為猴麵包樹的芽長得跟玫瑰的幼芽很像，一旦我看出它們和玫瑰的幼芽長得不一樣，就得立刻拔除它們，這工作雖然很無聊，卻相當簡單。」

有一天，他建議我，為我星球的小孩畫一張漂亮的圖。「如果他們去旅行時可能會有用處，」他又說：「有時候，把工作拖到最後再做也沒關係，可是像猴麵包樹這麼危險的植物，拖到最後一定會有大災難。我知道有一個行星上，住著一個懶傢伙，他根本就懶得管那三顆小種子……」

　　因此我依照小王子的建議，畫了懶傢伙居住的星球。我不喜歡說教，但對於猴麵包樹的危險性我們知道得太少，對於一個漫遊小行星的人來說，那是很危險的。

　　於是在這一生中，我第一次呼籲：「孩子們，小心猴麵包樹！」我真的很努力地畫出這幅畫，這樣我就可以警告和我一樣的朋友，因為他們從來都不知道需要對抗這種危險。

　　這張畫給我們的啓示值得我不厭其煩地這麼做。也許你會問，「為什麼在這本書裡，找不出任何一張像猴麵包樹這樣，令人印象深刻的畫？」答案很簡單：我盡力了，即使沒有每一張都成功──只有在畫猴麵包樹的時候，我整個人才被一種急切的心情催促著。

猴麵包樹

第 6 章

啊！小王子……我開始一點一滴地了解你憂鬱的小生命。你曾有一段時間，唯一的樂趣是欣賞夕陽。第四天的早晨，當你說：

「我喜歡看夕陽。走，我們一起去看太陽下山……」

「可是，我們必須等待……」

「等什麼？」

「等太陽下山哪！」

起初，你看起來好像很驚訝，接著忍不住笑了，「我一直以為我還在家裡。」

大家都知道，美國正午的時候，正是法國夕陽西下的時候。如果你能在一分鐘內到達法國，你就可以看到夕陽，不幸的是，法國太遠了。而在小王子的星球上，你需要做的只是把椅子向後挪一點，那你任何時候都可以看到夕陽。

「有一天，我看了四十四次夕陽！」

過了一會兒，小王子補充說：

「你知道的——當你真的感到很悲傷時，你就會喜歡看夕陽……」

「你看了四十四次夕陽的那天很悲傷嗎？」

小王子沒有回答。

第 7 章

　　第五天，我發現小王子的另一個祕密——再次感謝那隻羊。他突然問了我一個他沉思已久的問題。

　　「羊會吃灌木叢，也會吃花嗎？」

　　「羊找到什麼就吃什麼。」

　　「有刺的花也吃嗎？」

　　「是啊，有刺的花也吃。」

　　「那麼那些刺有什麼用？」

　　我不知道。當時我正忙著將一個卡在引擎上的螺絲拆下來。飛機損壞的情形蠻嚴重的，而當我的飲用水也漸漸用光時，我開始害怕最糟的情況要發生了。

　　「那些刺有什麼用呢？」

　　小王子一旦提出疑問，就絕不放棄，而我正為了螺絲生氣，於是不加思索地回答他：「刺一點用處也沒有。那是花朵用來表達恨意的！」

　　「噢！」

　　安靜了一會兒之後，小王子不滿地說：「我不相信！花很嬌弱、很單純。她們會盡全力保護自己，她們認為有刺會令人害怕……」

我沒有回答，那時自顧自地想：「如果這個螺絲轉不動的話，我就得拿一把槌子把它敲震出來。」

小王子又再次擾亂我的思緒：「所以，你想，花……」

「噢！不！」我大叫道：「不要！不要再問了！我什麼都不知道。我只是想到什麼就說什麼。你沒看到我正為了重要的事在忙嗎？」

他瞪著我，愣住了。

「重要的事！」

我的手正握著榔頭，手指污黑地沾滿引擎油，蹲在他眼中看來醜得要命的東西面前……

「你跟那些大人沒什麼兩樣！」

我覺得有點慚愧。然而，他卻無情地繼續說：「你們把每件事都弄混亂……每件事都弄得亂七八糟……」

他氣極了，一頭金髮在風中擺動。

「我知道有顆星球住了一位紅臉紳士。他從沒聞過花香，也沒看過星星，更沒愛過別人。他除了算數以外，就沒做過別的事，他跟你一樣，整天不斷地說：『我正在忙重要的事。』而且，他還驕傲得要命！他根本就算不上是個人——他只是一個蘑菇！」

「一個什麼？」

「一個蘑菇！」

小王子氣得臉色發白。

　　「幾百萬年來，花朵生來就有刺；就像幾百萬年來羊都在吃花一樣。難道去瞭解花身上為什麼會有這些沒用的刺，不重要嗎？花和羊之間的戰爭不重要嗎？這些事難道不比臃腫的紅臉紳士的數字更重要嗎？如果我知道——世界上唯一的一朵花，只長在我的星球上；而一隻羊卻在某天早上，一口就把她吃掉，而牠自己一點也不明白自己在做什麼——你居然覺得這不重要！」

　　他臉色漸漸轉紅，繼續說：「假如有人愛著一朵獨一無二，盛開在浩瀚星海裡的花，那當他抬頭仰望繁星時便會心滿意足。他可以告訴自己：『我心愛的花在那裡，就在那顆星球上……』但如果羊把花吃掉了，對他來說，所有的星光便會在剎那間消失了！而你竟然覺得這不重要！」

　　他說不下去，突然間流下淚來。

　　黑夜翩然而至，我放下手中的工具，槌子、螺絲、飢餓，甚至是死亡，對我都已不再重要。

　　在一顆星星，一顆星球，我的行星，地球上，有一位需要安慰的小王子。我將他擁入懷中，輕輕地搖晃他。我說，「你心愛的那朵花不會有危險，我幫你的羊畫個口罩；替你的花畫個護欄……我……」

　　我不知道該對他說些什麼，只覺得自己很笨拙。我不知道該如何才能和他一樣，不知道該如何再次與他交心。眼淚就是這麼奇妙的東西。

第 8 章

　　很快地，我對小王子說的那朵花瞭解得更多了。在小王子的星球上，花兒一向簡單，只有一圈花瓣；既不占空間，也不會打擾任何人；清晨綻放於草地上，傍晚就凋謝。然而有一天，不知從哪裡來的一顆種子，小王子非常仔細地觀察它，因為這株芽跟他以前看過的嫩芽都不一樣。

　　這可能是新品種的猴麵包樹。沒多久，這小株植物就停止生長，準備開花。小王子剛好看到這個巨形花苞長大，知道不尋常的事要發生了。這朵花仍舊在她綠色的身體裡裝扮自己，她精心挑選顏色，並逐一調整花瓣的角度，她不想成為一朵皺巴巴的罌粟花。她想開出整朵花苞的美麗。噢！是的！她是迷人的！她花了好幾天準備，然後某天早晨，就在日出之時，終於將她之前所隱藏的一切完全展現。

　　她經過這番精心裝扮，打著哈欠說：「啊……我還沒睡醒呢！花瓣還很凌亂……」

　　小王子發出少有的讚嘆：「妳好美！」

　　「可不是嘛？」花朵回答：「我還是和太陽同時出生的呢……」

小王子知道這朵花一點也不謙虛，可是她是多麼的迷人哪！

　　「我想現在是早餐時間，」她補充道，「我在想，如果你夠仁慈，明白我的需求──」

　　小王子慚愧地走了出去，替她提了一整壺水過來。

很快地,她虛榮心發作,開始折磨小王子。

譬如有一天,她對小王子說:「我不怕老虎,更不怕牠們的爪子。」

「我的星球上沒有半隻老虎,」小王子回應,「而且老虎也不喜歡吃草。」

「我才不是草呢!」花朵溫柔地說。

「對不起……」

「我不怕老虎,不過我沒辦法忍受風。你可以準備屏風吧?」

「不能忍受風,對一株植物來說真是不幸。」小王子內心想著,「就一朵花而言,她可真難理解……」

「晚上的時候我想待在玻璃罩裡。這個地方可真冷,我從前住的地方——」

但她止住不再往下說,因為她來到這時也只不過是顆種子,根本就不會知道其他地方。

這個愚蠢的謊言讓她感到很糗,於是她咳嗽了兩三聲,試圖轉移小王子的注意力。

「屏風呢?」

「我正要去找屏風,但是妳剛剛還在跟我說話呀!」

　於是她乾脆再多咳幾下，如此一來，小王子可能會感到愧疚。

　雖然小王子仍全心全意地關心花兒，但不久就不太相信她了。他把花朵無心的批評想得太嚴重，使他變得很不快樂。

　「我真不該在意她的話，」有一天，他告訴我：「不應該在意花說些什麼的，只要觀賞她們，聞聞花香就夠了。我的花使我整個星球都滿溢香氣，可是我卻不懂得享受那美好。那個利爪的故事，反而讓我感到不安，我本來應該是充滿溫柔和憐憫……」

他對我傾吐祕密。

　　「我根本就不了解我的花！我應該看的是她的行為舉止，而不是在意她說的話。她的香氣讓我的生活更加多采多姿，我真不該離開她的……我早該猜到，她那可笑小把戲背後的情感啊。花朵都是這麼自相矛盾！但我那時畢竟太年輕了，不知該如何去愛她。」

第 9 章

　　我認為小王子是利用候鳥遷移時逃走的。他準備離開的那天早上，把星球上的一切都整理得井然有序。他小心地清理活火山——他有兩座活火山，它們在他做早餐時很有用；他還有一座死火山，但是照小王子的想法，「誰也不知道會發生什麼事！」為了預防萬一，他把死火山也清理了。如果火山被整理得很乾淨，就會穩定且緩慢地燃燒，也不會突然爆發。火山爆發和煙囪著火一樣。

顯然在地球上，人類太渺小了，無法清理火山，這就是為什麼火山爆發，常常為我們帶來麻煩。

小王子那時帶著些許哀傷，拔起最後一根猴麵包樹的幼苗。他相信自己不會再回去了，在最後那個早晨，所有該做的例行公事，對他而言似乎都變得相當珍貴。當他最後一次為花兒澆水，並且準備用玻璃罩罩住花兒的時候，他突然覺得好想哭。

「再見！」他對花兒說。

但是花兒沒有回話。

「再見！」他又說了一次。

花兒咳了一聲，但她並沒有感冒。

「我一直都很傻，」她終於開口了，「我覺得很抱歉。請你試著快樂起來好嗎？」

他覺得很驚訝，花兒竟然沒有罵他。他十分困惑，拿著玻璃罩站在那兒，他無法理解她這種冷靜的情緒。

「我是愛你的，真的！」花兒告訴他：「你卻不知道。是我的錯……不過那不重要了。你一直都跟我一樣傻。快樂起來吧……把玻璃罩放到旁邊去，我不再需要它了。」

「那麼，風──」

「我還不至於那麼冷……夜裡的冷空氣對我有好處的，我是一朵花啊。」

「可是，動物──」

「哦，如果我想跟蝴蝶交朋友的話，當然就得忍受兩三隻毛毛蟲的拜訪囉。我聽說蝴蝶長得很漂亮。況且，如果沒有蝴蝶、沒有毛毛蟲，還會有誰來看我呢？你離我那麼遠……至於一些大型的動物，我才不怕呢，我有我的利爪啊。」

她天真地展示了身上的四根刺，然後說：

「別再那樣傻傻地站著！既然你已經決定要走，就快走吧！」

因為她不想讓小王子看到她哭泣。她是這樣一朵驕傲
的花……

第 10 章

　　小王子發現自己的星球附近還有——小行星編號 325，326，327，328，329，330，所以他開始一個一個拜訪它們，增廣見聞。

　　第一個小行星上住了一個國王。這位國王身著貴重的紫色貂皮長袍，坐在樣式簡單卻散發權威的寶座上。

　　「啊！來了一位子民！」國王看到小王子便如此大喊。

　　「他從沒見過我，怎麼會認得我？」小王子心想。

　　小王子不知道對國王來說，這個世界相當簡單，他將自己以外的人都當作子民。

　　「靠近一點，讓我好好把你看清楚點。」國王得意地說。他覺得自己終於成為「某人」的國王了。

　　小王子四處張望著，想找地方坐下，然而整個星球都被國王那件巨大的貂皮長袍蓋住了。所以，他只好繼續挺直站著。因為很累，他便打了個呵欠。

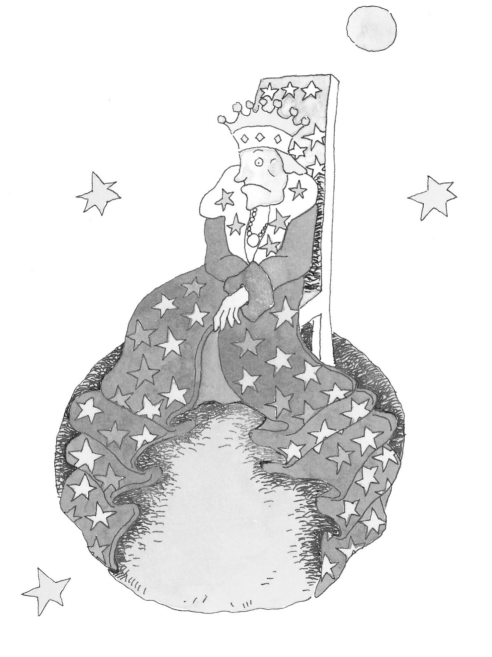

「在國王面前打呵欠是相當失禮的。」國王說，「我禁止打呵欠。」

小王子覺得很困惑，「我沒辦法停止呀！」他回答：「我長途跋涉來到這裡，睡眠不足……」

「噢，好，」國王說道。「那我就命令你打呵欠。我已經好久好久沒看過人打呵欠了。打呵欠可是很少見的。過來！再打個呵欠！這是命令。」

「這太為難我了……我無法再打一次呵欠……」小王子非常難為情地喃喃說著。

「嗯！那麼……」國王回答，「我 —— 我命令你有時打呵欠，有時 —— 呃……」

國王結巴了，並且有些惱怒。因為國王堅持他的權威必須受到尊重。他無法忍受別人抗命，不過他是如此和善，所以身為一個統治者，他只下合理的命令。

「如果我命令一個將軍變成一隻海鳥，」國王經常這樣解釋，「但他不聽我的命令，那並不是將軍的錯，而是我的錯。」

「我可以坐下嗎？」小王子怯怯地問。

「我命令你坐下。」國王回答道，把他威風的貂皮斗篷推到一邊。

然而，小王子覺得很疑惑……這個行星這麼小，國王能統治什麼？

「陛下，」小王子對國王說，「對不起，我想問問題 ——」

「我命令你問。」國王迅速地說。

「陛下,您統治什麼呢?」

「每一樣東西。」國王極為英明且簡潔地回答。

「每一樣東西?」

國王比了個手勢,意思是他的行星、其他行星,以及所有星球。

「您比的全部都是?」小王子問道。

「我比的全部都是。」國王回答。

因為他不僅是一位國王,還是一位宇宙的國王。

「那,星星也都聽命於您囉?」

「它們當然都聽我的,」國王說道,「而且是唯命是從!我不能忍受抗命。」

這樣的能力使小王子很驚訝。如果他能夠在同一天裡,不只看四十四次,而是看七十二次,或者一百次,甚至是二百次夕陽——根本不用移動椅子的話。

他想到他那顆被遺棄的小行星,小王子不自覺哀傷起來。他鼓起勇氣,請求國王幫他一個忙。

「我想看夕陽……您可以命令太陽下山,讓我開心嗎?」

「如果我命令一個將軍從一朵花飛到另一朵花,像蝴蝶一樣;或是叫他寫齣悲劇;或是叫他變成一隻海鳥,而將軍卻不遵照命令的話,我跟將軍,是誰錯了?」

「是您錯了。」小王子簡短地回答。

「對！我們不應該要求別人去做他們能力以外的事情，」國王繼續說道，「權威的主要根據是合理。如果你下令叫子民去跳海，就會發生革命。我有權要求我的子民服從命令，因為我的命令都是合理的。」

「那我的夕陽呢？」小王子提醒著，他從不會忘記他提出的問題。

「你會得到你的夕陽！我會十分堅持這件事。但是，根據我政治學的知識判斷，我得等待適當的時機。」

「那會是什麼時候？」小王子問。

「呃！呃！」國王邊回答邊翻閱一本巨大的年鑑。「讓我看看……那會是……大概……會是……今天晚上七點四十分左右。到時候你就可以親眼看到，萬物是如何遵從我的命令！」

小王子打了個呵欠。他很遺憾他等不到夕陽，他已經感到有點無聊。

「在這裡我沒有別的事可做，」他對國王說：「我要走了。」

「不要走。」因為好不容易有了子民，而感到驕傲的國王說：「不要走，我可以讓你當上大臣。」

「什麼大臣？」

「司——司法大臣。」

「可是這裡沒有什麼人需要審判啊！」

「這可不一定，」國王說，「我還沒有遊遍我的領土呢！我年紀大了，這裡沒地方可以放馬車，走路又會讓我疲倦。」

「喔，可是我已經全看過了！」小王子邊說邊彎下身，瀏覽星球的另一側。「那邊也沒有半個人……」

「這樣的話……」國王回答：「那你就審判你自己好了。這可是最困難的。審判自己要比審判別人難得多。如果你能成功做好這件事，你就是一個具有真正智慧的人。」

「你說得對，」小王子說：「但是我在哪都可以審判自己，沒必要留在這裡。」

「嗯！嗯！」國王說道，「我相信我的星球上住了一隻很老的老鼠，我晚上都會聽到牠的聲音。這樣吧，你可以審判牠呀！你可以每次都判牠死刑，牠的死活就看你如何審判。不過，每次你都必須再赦免牠，因為牠是這裡唯一的一隻老鼠。」

「我不喜歡審判任何人，」小王子說：「我該走了。」

國王大叫：「不！」

小王子不想傷老國王的心，所以當他準備離開時，他告訴國王：「如果陛下要我立刻奉命行事，你可以下達一個合理的命令，像是 —— 您下令我在一秒鐘內離開；而這是最好的……」

國王沒有回話，小王子嘆口氣，遲疑了一下，然後離開了。

「我會封你為大使！」國王趕緊在他的後面大喊。

國王擺出一副很權威的模樣。

「大人們真的很奇怪。」在他的旅程中，小王子這樣想著。

第11章

在第二個行星上，住了一個驕傲自大的男人。

「啊！太好了！有位崇拜者來拜訪我了！」當他一看到小王子時，就開始大聲嚷嚷。

對於驕傲自大的人來說，除了他以外的人都是崇拜者。

「早安！」小王子說：「你戴的帽子好奇怪！」

「這是為了答謝別人的稱讚。」驕傲自大

的人說，「當人們鼓掌時，我就會脫帽致意。不幸的是，從來沒有人經過這裡。」

「噢！」小王子不懂這個男人在講些什麼。

「快點拍手。」驕傲自大的人說。

小王子於是拍手；然後這個驕傲自大的男人就脫下帽子，謙虛地鞠躬。

「這比先前拜訪的那位國王好玩多了。」小王子又多拍了幾次手。驕傲自大的男人也再度脫帽致意。

玩了五分鐘後，小王子開始厭倦這個無聊的遊戲。

「要怎麼做，你的帽子才會掉下來？」小王子問。

但這個驕傲自大的人沒有回應，驕傲自大的人只聽得見讚美。

「你真的很崇拜我嗎？」他問小王子。

「崇拜是什麼意思？」

「崇拜的意思，就是你認為我是這個星球上最帥、穿得最漂亮、最有錢、而且最聰明的人⋯⋯」

「可是，你的星球上就只有你啊！」

「你就幫我一個忙，崇拜我一下嘛。」

「噢！」小王子聳聳肩，「我崇拜你。」但小王子覺得這件事一點也不有趣。

所以，他離開了。

「大人還真的是很奇怪！」他在旅程中如此想著。

第 12 章

第三個星球上住著
一位酒鬼。這次的拜
訪相當短暫，卻
使小王子陷入好
一陣子的沮喪。

「你在做什麼？」當小
王子發現酒鬼正坐在一堆空酒瓶及滿酒
瓶之間，這麼問他。

「喝酒啊！」酒鬼悶悶不樂地說。

「為什麼？」小王子追問。

「為了遺忘。」酒鬼回答。

「遺忘什麼？」小王子問的當下都替他感到難
過了。

「為了遺忘我很可恥。」酒鬼垂頭懺悔著。

「為什麼可恥？」小王子覺得他需要幫助。

「因為我喝酒！」酒鬼一說完，就醉倒在一片寂靜中。

小王子帶著滿心的困惑離開。

「大人們真是非常、非常的奇怪。」他在旅程中這樣想著。

第 13 章

　　第四個星球是屬於一個商人的。這個商人相當忙碌，忙到連小王子抵達時，頭也沒抬一下。

　　「早安，」小王子和他打招呼：「你的香煙熄了。」

　　「三加二等於五；五加七等於十二；十二加三等於十五。早安！十五加七等於二十二；二十二加六等於二十八。我沒時間再點煙了。二十六加五等於三十一。哇！總共是五億零一百六十二萬二千七百三十一。」

　　「五億什麼？」小王子問。

　　「什麼？你怎麼還在這？五億零一百萬 ── 呃……我忘了。我不能停下來……我很忙！我只關心重要的事。二加五等於七……」

　　「五億零一百萬什麼？」小王子重覆道。只要他問了問題，就絕對不放棄。

　　商人抬起頭。

　　「我在這行星住了五十四年，這中間只被打斷過三次。第一次是二十二年前，不曉得從哪來了一隻甲蟲，發出惱人的噪音，害我算錯四次。第二次是十一年前，我的風溼病發作。都怪我運動量不夠，也沒時間散步。第三次——嗯，就是現在！我剛剛說到哪裡了？五億零一百萬——」

「五億零一百萬什麼？」

這個商人意識到他如果不回答，就不可能得到寧靜。

「那些小東西，就是你常在天空看到的那些。」

「蒼蠅嗎？」

「不，不是，就是小小的發光物。」

「蜜蜂嗎？」

「噢，不是。就是小小的、金光閃閃的東西，那些讓懶惰人做白日夢的東西。不過，我只能關心重要的事情，我才沒時間做白日夢！」

「哦！你是指星星？」

「對！就是星星。」

「你為什麼要五億顆星星？」

「是五億零一百六十二萬二千七百三十一顆星星。我可是相當關心重要的事，所以計算結果是非常精確的。」

「那你要這些星星做什麼用？」

「這些星星做什麼用？」

「對啊。」

「沒怎麼用啊。我擁有它們。」

「哦，你擁有這些星星？」

「是啊。」

「可是，我剛遇到一個國王，他──」

「國王並沒有擁有權，國王統治它們，這是不一樣的意思！」

「可是，你擁有這些星星有什麼用呢？」

「它讓我變得很有錢。」

「有錢有什麼用？」

「那我就可以買更多星星，只要有新的星星被發現的話。」

「這個人的邏輯跟那個酒鬼一樣……」小王子心想。

但是不管如何，小王子還有其他問題：「人怎麼能擁有星星呢？」

「那還有誰可以擁有它們？」商人焦躁地反駁。

「我不知道，沒有人吧?!」

「那就對了！它們就是我的，因為我是第一個想擁有它們的人。」

「這樣就可以嗎？」

「當然。如果你發現一顆沒有主人的鑽石，它就是你的；當你發現一座無人小島，那座島就是你的；當你比別人早一點想到任何創意，然後去申請專利，那就是你的。現在這些星星歸我所有，因為之前從來沒人想過要擁有星星！」

「你說得很有道理。」小王子說道。「那要用它們做什麼呢？」

「我管理它們。」商人回答，「我正在重覆計算它們的數量。這相當困難，不過我只關心重要的事情。」

　　小王子仍然不滿意。

　　「如果我有一條圍巾，我就會把它圍在脖子上；如果我有一朵花，我可以把它摘下來帶走。可是，你不能把星星摘下來……」

　　「是不行，但是，我可以把它們放在銀行。」

　　「那是什麼意思？」

　　「意思就是，我可以把我有多少星星的數字寫在一張紙上，然後把這張紙鎖在抽屜裡。」

　　「這樣就好了嗎？」

　　「這樣就可以了。」商人說道。

　　「真好玩。」小王子想。「這樣做是有點詩意，但一點也不重要嘛。」小王子對於什麼事情是重要的，跟大人們的觀點非常不一樣。

　　他繼續對商人說：「我自己擁有一朵花，我每天幫她澆水；我有三座火山，我每個禮拜都會清理一次，以防萬一，我也清理死火山。對我的花和火山來說，我是有用處的。可是，你對星星來說似乎沒有用處……」

　　商人張大嘴巴，想不到可以說什麼，然後小王子就走了。

　　「大人們真的非常奇怪。」小王子單純地這樣想著，繼續他的旅程。

第 14 章

　　第五顆星球真的很奇特。它是所有星球中最小的，只有容納一支燈柱和一位點燈夫的空間。

　　小王子無法理解，在宇宙裡，一個沒人居住也沒有房子的星球上，為什麼需要燈柱和點燈夫？然而，他告訴自己：

　　「這個點燈夫也許很不尋常，但比起國王、驕傲自大的人、商人及酒鬼好多了。至少他的工作有意義。當他點亮街燈時，就好像賦予一顆星星或花朵生命一樣；當他熄掉街燈時，就像是送星星或花朵回去安眠。這是個美好又有用的工作。」

　　他懷著崇敬點燈夫的心情，登上這個星球。

　　「早安，為什麼你剛剛把燈熄掉了呢？」

　　「這是規則，」點燈夫回答：「早安。」

　　「你的規則是什麼？」

　　「把燈熄掉！晚安。」點燈夫再次把燈點亮。

　　「可是，為什麼你剛剛又把燈點亮？」

　　「規則呀。」點燈夫回答。

「我不懂。」小王子說道。

「沒什麼好懂的，」點燈夫說：「規則就是規則。早安。」

於是，他再次把燈熄了。

接著他用一條紅格紋手帕擦擦額頭。

「我這個工作真的很辛苦。以前很合理，我只要在早上把燈熄掉，傍晚再點上就好了。我有一整天的時間可以休息，一整晚的時間可以睡覺。」

「後來規則變了嗎？」

「規則沒變。」點燈夫回答。「問題就在這裡。星球運轉的速度愈來愈快，而規則卻沒變！」

「所以呢？」小王子問。

「所以現在這個星球一分鐘運轉一次，我真的是一刻也不能休息！我得在一分鐘內點燈、熄燈！」

「真有趣！你的一天只維持一分鐘而已。」

「一點都不有趣！」點燈夫說道。「我們已經對談一個月了。」

「我們嗎？」

「對啊，一個月、三十分鐘、三十天了，晚安。」

點燈夫又把燈點亮。

小王子看著點燈夫如此忠於自己的工作，真心地喜歡他。小王子想起自己以前只要把椅子往後挪就可以看到日落，於是他想幫助點燈夫。

「你知道嗎？」小王子說，「有一個方法可以讓你休息，當你想休息的時候……」

「我一直都想休息。」點燈夫說：「一個人是不可能同時努力工作又偷懶的。」

小王子繼續說：「你的星球這麼小，只要走三步就可以繞一圈，所以你必須走慢點，停留在陽光下就好了；當你想休息時你可以開始走路，想要白天有多長就有多長。」

「那對我來說沒什麼用，」點燈夫說，「我這一生中最愛的是睡覺。」

「你可真是不幸。」小王子說。

「是啊，」燈夫說，「早安。」他把燈熄掉。

小王子繼續踏上他的旅程，他獨自想著：「國王、驕傲自大的人、酒鬼、商人一定都會看不起點燈夫。然而，他卻是我唯一不覺得他愚蠢的人。也許因為他是唯一不為自己而忙碌的人吧！」

他感慨地嘆了口氣，再度自言自語：「他是唯一一個我想跟他做朋友的人。可他的行星實在太小了，根本沒地方容納兩個人……」

然而，小王子卻不敢承認，他對於離開這個星球，感到特別難過的原因——這個星球上每二十四小時有一千四百四十次夕陽。

第 15 章

　　第六個星球是上個星球的十倍大。這裡住著一位老先生，他正在寫一本很厚重的書。

　　「哇！探險家來了！」當他看到小王子時，不由得大叫。

　　小王子氣喘吁吁的在桌子面前坐下，他的旅程有點遠了。

　　「你從哪兒來？」老先生問道。

　　「那本厚厚的書是什麼呢？」小王子問：「你在做什麼？」

　　「我是一名地理學家。」老先生回答。

　　「地理學家是什麼？」

　　「地理學家就是一個了解海洋、河川、城鎮、山脈及沙漠等位置的專家。」

　　「真有趣，」小王子說：「終於有一個專家了。」他開始環顧地理學家的星球，發現這是他看過最宏偉的星球。

　　「你的星球真是漂亮，有海洋嗎？」

「我不知道。」地理學家說道。

「哦!」小王子:「那有山脈嗎?」

「我不知道。」地理學家回答。

「那城市、河流、沙漠呢?」

「這些我都不知道。」

「但你是一名地理學家啊!」

「是啊,」地理學家說道,「但我不是探險家啊。我這兒根本沒有探險家。地理學家是不需要去計算和探測城鎮、河流、高山、大海、大洋、沙漠的。地理學家的工作太重要了,根本不能在外面閒晃!他是絕不能離開書桌的,不過,他會從探險家那兒接收資訊做為研究材料。他會問他們問題,記錄他們的經歷。要是某位探險家提供的旅遊記錄過分有趣,那地理學家就會調查他的品行。」

「為什麼?」

「一名說謊探險家會讓地理學家寫的書變糟!飲酒過量的探險家也是一樣。」

「為什麼?」

「因為酒醉的人會看到雙重影像啊。所以地理學家會把原本只有一座山的地方標示成兩座。」

「我認識一個人,他可能就是這種探險家。」小王子說。

「可能是這樣。所以如果一個探險家的品行似乎還不錯,他的發現就得好好地調查一番。」

「你會跑去那些地方察看嗎？」

「不，那太複雜了。可以要求探險家必須提出一些證據。譬如，探險家發現一座大山，他就得把山上的大石頭搬回來才行。」

地理學家突然變得興奮。

「不過──你來自遙遠的地方！你是探險家！你必須描述你的行星給我聽！」

地理學家打開他的紀錄冊，削尖他的鉛筆。

「探險家的敘述一開始是用鉛筆寫，等探險家把證據帶回來以後，才會用鋼筆寫下來。」

　　「說吧！」地理學期待地問。

　　「噢，我住的地方不是很有趣，」小王子說，「它很小。我有三座火山——兩座活火山、一座死火山，雖然不知道它會不會再次爆發。」

　　「你當然不會知道。」地理學家說。

　　「我還有一朵花。」

　　「我們對花不感興趣。」地理學家說。

　　「為什麼？那是我的星球上最美的東西啊！」

　　「因為花不列入記錄，」地理學家說，「因為花朵是『朝生暮死』的。」

　　「什麼是『朝生暮死』？」

　　「地理學書籍是所有事物中最重要的，」地理學家說道，「它們永遠不會褪流行。一座山幾乎不太會移動；而海洋也不太可能乾涸，我們記載的是永恆的事物。」

　　「可是，死火山也可能再度活起來啊，」小王子問：「『朝生暮死』是什麼意思？」

　　「對我們來說，不論死火山或活火山都一樣。」地理學家說道。「我們在意的只是山，而山是不會移動的。」

　　「但是，『朝生暮死』是什麼意思？」小王子又問。在他的一生中，只要他開始問問題就不會放棄。

　　「就是『註定很快消失』的意思。」

「我的花註定很快消失？」

「那當然。」

「我的花是朝生暮死的，」小王子心想，「而且她只有四根刺保護自己、對抗外界。我竟然將她獨自留在星球上！」

這是小王子第一次對自己的離開感到懊悔。不過，他很快地再次振奮精神。

「你建議我下一站去哪兒呢？」他問。

「地球，」地理學家回答：「它的名聲不錯。」

於是小王子離開了，心中想念著他的花。

第 16 章

　　地球真不是一個普通的星球！有一百一十一位國王（當然，也包括黑人國王在內）、七千位地理學家、九十萬個商人、七百五十萬個酒鬼，還有三億一千一百萬個驕傲自大的人──這些全部加起來，大約有二十億個大人。

　　為了讓你對地球的大小有概念，我可以告訴你，在發明電燈之前，如果要點亮全球六大洲的話，就得勞動四十六萬二千五百一十一個點燈夫來點燈。

　　從遠方看，這會是相當壯觀的場面。這群點燈大隊的動作排列大概會和芭蕾舞一樣整齊。

　　首先上場點燈的應該是紐西蘭和澳洲的點燈夫，點完燈便退回去，睡覺；接著，就換中國和西伯利亞的點燈夫，從大隊中出場，接著很快就退回去；然後輪到蘇俄和印度的點燈夫；隨後是非洲和歐洲；再來是南美洲和北美洲的點燈夫。而且不會有人弄錯出場的順序，這真是一個奇觀啊！

　　唯一可以過得比較輕鬆的點燈夫，只有負責北極孤燈和南極孤燈的點燈夫，他們一年只要工作兩次就可以了。

第 17 章

　　當你試著想詼諧地說故事時，就會發現你自己會撒點無關緊要的小謊。我並沒有完全真實地告訴你點燈夫的事。我可能會讓那些不清楚地球現狀的人，留下錯誤的印象。人們在地球上所占據的空間其實很小；如果將地球上二十億人像參加聚會般緊密地排在一起，他們很容易就能擠進一個邊長三十二公里的正方形廣場。所有人類都能擠進一個太平洋的小島。

　　你跟大人們說這件事他們絕對不相信。他們覺得自己占了很大的空間，以為自己跟猴麵包樹一樣重要。你可以告訴他們重要的事就是計算數字。他們喜歡數字，也樂在其中。但可別特別花時間做這件事，這一點也不必要。相信我。

　　小王子一登陸就很驚訝，因為他沒看到任何人。當一個月光色的東西在沙間移動時，他已經在猜：自己是不是登陸錯星球了。

　　「晚安。」小王子並不指望得到回答。

　　「晚安。」蛇說。

「我在哪一個星球？」小王子問。

「在地球上、在非洲。」蛇回答。

「哦！地球上難道沒有人嗎？」

「這是沙漠，沙漠中是沒有人的。地球是很大的。」蛇說。

小王子在一個石頭上坐下來，仰望天空。

「我在想，星星們閃閃發亮是不是為了要讓每個人都找得到自己的星球，」他說：「看看我的星球，它就在我們頭頂上，距離卻如此遙遠！」

「真是個美麗的星球。」蛇說，「你為什麼會來這裡？」

「我和一朵花之間有點問題。」小王子說。

「噢！」蛇說。

他們倆沉默了一會兒。

「所有的人都去哪兒了？」小王子再度開口：「在沙漠裡有點寂寞呢。」

「在人群裡也會感到寂寞的。」蛇說。

小王子凝視蛇很長一段時間。

「你是個有趣的生物。」他說，「只跟我的手指一樣粗……」

「可是，我比國王的手指頭還要有力。」蛇說。

小王子微笑了。

「你才沒有什麼力呢！你又沒有腳，也走不了多遠……」

「我可以帶你去比任何船隻航程都更遠的地方。」
蛇說。

牠把自己纏在小王子的腳踝上，就像一只金鐲子一樣。

「地球上無論是誰被我碰到，就會被我送回老家，」牠
繼續說，「可是，你是如此純潔，又來自某個星球……」

小王子沒有回答。

「我為你感到難過——在這個花崗岩組成的地球上，你
是如此脆弱，」蛇說，「如果你發現自己很想家的話，我可
以幫助你……」

「噢！我完全了解你的意思，」小王子說：「可是，為
什麼你的話像是猜謎呢？」

「我專門解答謎題。」蛇說。

接著他倆陷入沉默。

第 18 章

　　小王子穿越沙漠，但他只遇到一朵花。那是一朵有著三個花瓣，看起來很普通的花。

　　「早安。」小王子說。
　　「早安。」花說。
　　「人們都在哪？」小王子有禮貌地問。

　　這朵花曾看到一隊商隊經過。

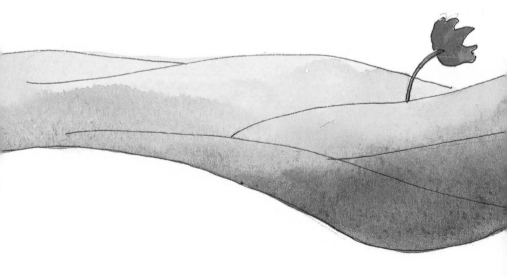

「人嗎？大概有六、七個吧，我想我幾年前看過他們，但是你找不到他們的。他們被風吹走了；你知道的，他們沒有根，生活很艱困。」

「再見了。」小王子說。

「再見。」花兒說。

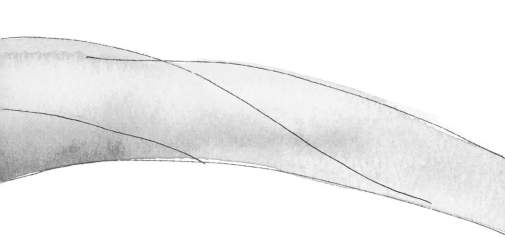

第 19 章

　　之後，小王子爬上一座高山。以前他認識的山，就只有他那到膝蓋左右的三座火山，他還習慣把死火山當做小椅子呢！他心想，「登上這麼高的一座山，我就可以一眼望盡整個星球和所有人了……」

　　然而，他可以看見的僅有尖銳的山峰群。

　　「你好！」他並不指望有任何回應。

　　「你好——你好——你好……」一個回音傳來。

　　「你是誰？」小王子問。

　　「你是誰——你是誰——你是誰……」回音回答。

　　「做我的朋友吧！我好寂寞。」他說。

　　「我好寂寞——我好寂寞——我好寂寞……」回音回答。

　　「好奇怪的星球！」小王子心想，「這裡又乾、又粗糙、又險惡，一點想像力都沒有，只會重覆別人對他們說的話……在我的星球上，我的花總是第一個說話……」

第 20 章

　　走過沙漠、岩地和雪地之後，小王子發現了一條路。道路旁有人居住著。

　　「你好。」他說。

　　他在一個玫瑰花園裡。

　　「你好。」玫瑰花們回答。

　　小王子凝視著她們，她們看起來都像是他的那一朵花。

　　「妳們是誰？」他驚訝地問。

　　「我們是玫瑰花呀。」玫瑰們說。

　　他覺得很傷心，他的花曾經告訴他，全宇宙只有她一朵玫瑰花。而光是這個花園裡就有五千朵玫瑰花，長得跟他的玫瑰花一模一樣！

　　「如果她看到這幅景像，她一定會氣得要命，」他心想，「她肯定會咳得很厲害，而且會裝出一副快死的樣子，以免被嘲笑。而我就得裝出照顧她的樣子 —— 因為如果我不這樣做的話，她真的會羞憤而死……」

　　然後他對自己說：「我以為我很富有，因為我擁有一朵

全宇宙獨一無二的花。當我所擁有的只是一朵普通的玫瑰
花，三座高度及膝的火山，其中一座還可能永遠都是死火
山……這些根本就不能讓我成為一個了不起的人……」

　　於是，小王子趴在草地上哭泣著。

第 21 章

　此時，狐狸出現了。

　「早安。」狐狸說。

　「早安。」小王子習慣性地禮貌回答。當他轉過頭，卻什麼也沒看到。

　「我在這，在蘋果樹下。」那個聲音說。

　「你是誰？」小王子問，並且補充了一句，「你看起來好漂亮。」

　「我是一隻狐狸。」狐狸說道。

　「和我一起玩吧！」小王子提議：「我現在心情很不好。」

　「我不能和你玩，」狐狸回答：「因為我還沒被馴服。」

　「啊！對不起。」小王子說。

　可是他想了一想，又問：「『馴服』是什麼意思？」

　「原來你不是這裡的人。」狐狸說。「你在找什麼？」

　「人類，」小王子說，「『馴服』是什麼意思？」

　狐狸說：「人類有槍，而且會打獵，真是討厭；不過他

們也養雞,這是他們的優點。你在找雞嗎?」

「不是,」小王子說,「我在找朋友。『馴服』是什麼意思?」

「就是常常被人們遺忘的事情,」狐狸說道,「它的意思是建立關係……」

「建立關係?」

「沒錯,」狐狸說:「對我而言,你只不過是個小男孩,就跟其他千百個小男孩一樣。而我不需要你,你也不需要我。對你而言,我只是隻狐狸而已,就跟其他千百隻狐狸一樣。不過如果你馴服我,我們將會需要彼此,對我而言,你將會是宇宙間獨一無二的。」

「我好像懂了……」小王子說，「有一朵花……我想她已經馴服我了……」

「很有可能，」狐狸說，「在地球上，任何事都會發生。」

「噢，這不是在地球上發生的事。」小王子說。

狐狸非常好奇：「在別的星球嗎？」

「是的。」

「那個星球有獵人嗎？」

「沒有。」

「哇，太棒了！那雞呢？」

「沒有。」

「果真沒有十全十美的事。」狐狸嘆了口氣。

但狐狸很快地又說：

「我的生活相當乏味，我獵捕雞，人類獵捕我，所有的雞都一樣，所有的人類也都一樣，所以我已經感到厭煩。假如你能馴服我，那我的生命就會充滿陽光，你的腳步聲會開始變得與眾不同。其他人的腳步聲會讓我迅速躲到地底下，但你的腳步聲會如音樂般呼喚我離開洞穴。你看到那邊的麥田了嗎？我不吃麵包，小麥對我來說一點用處也沒有。麥田無法讓我聯想到任何事，那真的很可悲。但是你有一頭金黃色的頭髮，假如你馴服我，那該有多棒啊！金黃色的麥子會讓我想起你，而我將會愛上風在麥穗間吹拂的聲音……」

狐狸停止說話，並且凝視著小王子。

「求求你——馴服我吧!」

「我很想,」小王子說,「可是我沒有太多時間。我想去交朋友,還有瞭解許多事情。」

「你只能瞭解你所馴服的東西。」狐狸說。「人類不會花時間去瞭解事情,他們會在商店裡買現成的東西,只是沒有任何一家店有販賣友誼。所以人類不再有朋友了。如果你要一個朋友,就馴服我吧!」

「那我要做些什麼事?」小王子問。

「你必須要很有耐心。」狐狸回答。「首先,你必須在稍遠的地方坐下來,像那裡的草地上。我會從眼角餘光看你,而你不能說話。言語會導致誤解。然後每天,你可以坐靠近我一點……」

第二天,小王子來了。

「你在同一時間過來會比較好。」狐狸說,「如果你在下午四點拜訪我,那三點的時候,我就會開始覺得快樂,接下來我就會愈來愈快樂。四點的時候,我就已經開始煩躁擔心了,那麼我將會知道快樂的真諦!如果你隨便在任何時間過來的話,我就不知道該怎麼在心裡做好迎接你的準備……一個人必須要有一些儀式。」

「什麼是儀式?」小王子問道。

「這是另一件經常被人們遺忘的事。」狐狸說。「儀式就是使某一天跟另一天有所不同,讓某一小時跟別的小時也有所不同的事。舉例來說,那些獵人有一種儀式,每週四他們都會和村裡的女孩跳舞，所以禮拜四就變得很特別，我會一直散步到葡萄園。如果獵人想在任何時候跳舞，所有的日子也就會變得一樣。我就不能休息了。」

　　因此當小王子馴服了狐狸，離別的時刻近了——

　　「噢，天哪！」狐狸說，「我快哭了。」

　　「這是你的錯啊，」小王子說。「我不想傷害你，是你要我馴服你的……」

　　「對啊。」狐狸說。

「但是，你快哭出來了！」小王子說。

「對啊。」狐狸說。

「那你根本沒得到什麼好處！」

「不！我有得到好處，因為現在我擁有麥子的顏色。」
他接著說：「再去看看玫瑰花吧！你就會知道，你的玫瑰花
是獨一無二的。再回來和我道別，我會告訴你一個祕密。」

於是，小王子離開去看玫瑰花。

「妳們一點兒也不像我的玫瑰。」他告訴她們，「妳們什麼也不是。沒有人馴服過妳們，妳們也沒馴服過任何人。妳們就和我當初遇見的狐狸一樣，牠曾經和其他千百隻狐狸相同，但現在牠是我的朋友了，對我而言，牠是世界上獨一無二的狐狸了。」

　　玫瑰們顯得不太高興。

　　「妳們很美，」他繼續說，「但是很空虛。沒有人會為妳們而死，沒錯，一般路人可能會認為我的玫瑰和妳們很像，但只要有她一朵就能勝過妳們全部。因為她是我灌溉的那朵玫瑰花，她是我放在玻璃罩裡，被我保護不被風吹襲，甚至為她打死毛毛蟲（只留兩、三隻變成蝴蝶）的玫瑰。她是那朵我願意傾聽她發牢騷、吹噓、甚至沉默的那朵玫瑰。因為，她是『我的』玫瑰。」

　　然後，小王子回到狐狸那裡。

　　「再見。」他說。

　　「再見。」狐狸說。「我的祕密——很簡單：『只有用心才能真的看見，真正重要的東西肉眼是看不見的。』」

　　「真正重要的東西肉眼是看不見的。」小王子重覆著狐狸的話，以防自己忘記。

　　「因為你為玫瑰花付出的時間，你的玫瑰花才會顯得如此重要。」

　　「因為我為她付出的時間……」小王子說著，以免自己忘記。

「人類已經忘記這個簡單的真理。」狐狸說，「不過你不可以忘記，你必須對你馴服的所有東西負責。你必須對你的玫瑰花負責……」

「我必須對我的玫瑰花負責。」小王子反覆唸著這些話，這樣他才不會忘記。

第 22 章

「你好！」小王子說道。

「你好！」鐵路號誌員回應。

「你在這裡做什麼？」小王子問。

「我將旅客們分成一千個一批，」鐵路號誌員說，「再把他們帶上火車，往右邊或往左邊送走。」

一列光亮的火車發出雷聲般的隆隆巨響，極速通過，它的燈一閃一閃，有如一條銀色的蛇。

「他們真忙啊。」小王子說，「他們要去哪裡呢？」

「恐怕連火車駕駛員也不知道吧！」鐵路號誌員回答。

一列光亮的急速火車，也隆隆作響地從反方向進站。

「他們已經回來了嗎？」小王子又問。

「這是不同的一批人。」鐵路號誌員回答，「這裡是鐵路交叉點。」

「他們不喜歡自己住的地方嗎？」小王子再問。

「沒有人會安於自己所在的環境。」鐵路號誌員回應。

第三列火車的隆隆聲已經傳來。

「他們在追第一批旅客，對不對？」小王子繼續問。

「他們什麼人也不追。他們在裡面睡覺、打呵欠。」鐵路號誌員說，「除了小孩子會把鼻子壓在玻璃窗上。」

「只有小孩子才知道他們在找什麼。」小王子說，「他們會付出時間在一個娃娃身上，那個娃娃就會變得很重要。如果有人把娃娃拿走，他們就會哭了……」

「是啊，孩子真幸運。」鐵路號誌員說道。

第 23 章

　　「早安。」小王子說。

　　「早安。」商人說。

　　這個商人專賣一種止渴的藥丸。一個星期吃一顆，你就可以不必喝水。

　　「你為什麼要賣這種藥丸呢？」小王子問。

　　「這種藥丸可以節省很多時間呀！」商人回答。「專家已經計算過，每星期可以節省五十三分鐘。」

　　「人們會怎麼運用那五十三分鐘？」

　　「他們愛怎麼用，就怎麼用。」

　　「如果我有空下來的五十三分鐘，」小王子說：「我會漫步到泉水邊。」

第 24 章

　　這是我在沙漠失事的第八天。當我正聽著小王子說商人的故事時，我也喝完最後一滴水了。

　　「噢，」我告訴小王子，「聽你敘述的冒險是很棒。不過我飛機還沒修好，而且現在水也一滴不剩了：『如果』可以，我很樂意散步到泉水邊！」

　　「我的朋友狐狸他──」小王子告訴我。

　　「孩子，你的那隻狐狸朋友，跟這件事沒什麼關係。」

　　「為什麼？」

　　「因為，我們就快要渴死了……」

　　他根本就不了解我的意思，於是繼續說：

　　「有個朋友很好，即使你快死了，像我就很高興，我『真的』擁有一個狐狸朋友……」

　　「他根本一點危機意識也沒有。」我提醒自己，「他根本就沒有渴過，也沒餓過，他所需要的只是一點陽光就可以了。」

　　他凝視著我，回答了我正在思考的問題：

「我也很渴，我們去找井吧……」

我疲倦地聳聳肩。在廣袤無垠的沙漠裡，想找到一口井是不可能的。然而，我們還是出發了。

我們沉默地走了數小時以後，黑夜降臨，星星升起。

我渴得有些神智不清，乍看星空，彷彿自己正置身夢中。小王子說過的話在我腦海中迴盪——

「你也口渴嗎？」我說。

他沒有回答我的問題，他只說：「水對心靈很有用……」

我不了解他的意思，只好沉默。我知道，人類絕不可以對他產生質疑。

他累了，於是他坐下來。我也坐在他身旁。

過了一會兒，他說：

「因為有一朵我們看不見的花，星星才顯得如此美麗。」

「嗯。」我默默地看著在月光下不斷綿延的沙堆。

「沙漠是如此的美麗。」小王子說。

這倒是真的。我一直很喜歡沙漠。你可以坐在沙丘上，即使看不到任何東西，也聽不見任何聲音；無聲中卻有某種東西散發出光芒……

「沙漠是因什麼而美麗呢？」小王子說，「是因為它不知在何處藏了一口井嗎？」

我相當驚訝，我突然理解他說的沙漠中的神祕光芒，當我還小的時候，我住在一棟古老的房子裡，傳說那裡埋有寶藏。當然，沒有人能找到寶藏，可能也沒有人看過寶藏。那房子卻因此籠罩著魔力。在我家的地心深處，埋藏了一個祕密……

「對，」我對小王子說，「不管是房子、星星，或是沙漠──都因為有看不見的東西而顯得美麗！」

「我很高興你同意我對狐狸的看法了。」他說。

當小王子沉浸夢中，我把他抱起來，再度出發。

我覺得很感動，彷彿我懷裡抱著一件易碎的珍寶。對我來說，世界上再也沒有比小王子更易碎的寶物了。

月光下，我看著他蒼白的額頭，緊閉的雙眼，微風中顫動的捲髮。我內心想：「我看到的不再是外觀而已，真正重要的是那些看不到的東西……」

他的雙唇半開，形成了一個微笑。

我再次想：「我之所以會對小王子這麼感動，是因為他對玫瑰花的忠誠──玫瑰花的存在讓他發光，就像是點燃的燈火，即便他睡著了……」

然後我覺得他似乎更易碎了。像燈火般需要被保護，一陣狂風就可以將它們吹熄。於是，我繼續向前走，直到天亮，我找到了一口井。

第 25 章

「人們拚命將自己擠進急速火車裡，」小王子說：「卻不知道自己在尋找什麼。於是他們變得憂慮煩躁，在原地打轉。」

然後他又補充道：「其實根本不值得……」

我們所找到的井不像沙漠的井。沙漠的井只是地上的洞，這個井卻像村莊的井。可是這四周並沒有村莊啊。我心想，我一定是在做夢……

「真奇怪，」我告訴小王子，「打水用具很齊全呢，滑輪、水桶、繩子。」

他笑了，拉起繩子，轉動滑輪。滑輪發出的聲音，如同無風吹動般的老舊風向標。

「你聽！」小王子說。「我們叫醒這口井了，它正在唱歌呢……」

我不希望小王子累死自己。

「讓我來吧！」我說，「這對你來說太重了。」

我慢慢地把水桶拉至我穩穩坐著的水井邊緣。滑輪的歌

聲仍然在耳際迴響，而顫動的水面還閃爍著粼粼波光。

「我好渴，好想喝水，」小王子說，「給我一點兒水喝……」

我明白他在找尋什麼了。

我把水桶舉到他唇邊，他閉著眼睛啜飲，彷彿飲用饗宴上的酒。這時候水變得不是一般普通的水，它來自星空下漫步、滑輪的歌聲和我打水的辛勞呢！它就像是一件禮物，慰藉我的心靈。當我還是小男孩時，聖誕樹上的光、午夜彌撒的音樂及溫柔的笑臉，都為我收到的禮物綻放出光芒。

「人類在一個花園裡種了五千朵玫瑰，」小王子說：「卻找不到真正想要的。」

「是啊，他們是沒找到。」我回答。

「其實他們要找的東西可能存在於一朵玫瑰和一口水中。」

「是啊，很有可能。」我說。

然後小王子接著說：

「雙眼是盲目的，我們必須用心體會才能看見。」

我已經喝過水，呼吸也順暢許多。旭日將沙漠染成蜂蜜色，我對這個顏色感到很快樂。然而，為什麼我的心頭又是如此憂傷？

「你一定要遵守諾言。」小王子溫柔地說，他再度在我身旁坐下。

「什麼諾言？」

「你知道的 —— 替我的羊畫口罩……我得對我的玫瑰花負責呀！」

我從口袋裡掏出我畫的草圖。小王子看看那些畫，然後笑著說：

「你的猴麵包樹看起來好像高麗菜。」

「喔！」

我本來還為我畫的猴麵包樹感到相當驕傲呢！

「你的狐狸耳朵畫得像角，而且它們太長了。」然後他又笑了。

「這不公平啊，我唯一會畫的就只有蟒蛇的外觀和透視圖。」

「噢，沒關係的，」他說，「小孩看得懂的。」

然後，我畫了一個口罩。當我把口罩交給他時，我的心跳似乎停止了。

「你有什麼計畫是我不知道的嗎？」

他沒有回答我，只說：

「你知道嗎，明天就是我到地球的週年紀念日了……」

經過短暫的沉默後，他繼續說：

「我降落的地方就在附近。」

然後他臉紅了。

再一次，不知道為什麼，我心頭又掠過一絲憂傷。突然間我想到一個問題：

「那一週前的早晨，我在罕無人跡的地方遇見你，並不是偶然？當時你準備回到你降落的地方？」

　　小王子的臉又紅了。

　　於是我有點猶豫地說：

　　「是因為週年紀念日的關係嗎？」

　　小王子再一次臉紅了。他沒有回答我的問題。但臉紅就表示「是」了，不是嗎？

　　「噢，」我說：「我好怕。」

　　他卻回答：「現在，你必須要回去工作了，快回去修飛機吧。我會一直在這裡，你明天傍晚再回來這裡……」

　　可是我放不下心。我想起了狐狸的話，如果你讓自己被馴服，就有可能會流淚……

第 26 章

　　水井旁有一座老舊傾塌的石牆。

　　當我隔天晚上修好飛機後趕過來時，從遠處就能看見小王子坐在牆上，兩隻腳晃來晃去。我聽到他說：

　　「你不記得了嗎，這裡不是正確地點。」

　　一定是誰在跟他說話，因為那聲音回答：

　　「是，是！是今天沒錯，但這裡不是正確的地點。」

　　我繼續朝著牆走去，仍然沒看到或聽見任何人的聲音。

　　但是，小王子再度說話了。

　　「——當然。你可以在沙漠上找到我最初的足跡。在那兒等我吧！我今晚會在那裡。」

　　我距離那片牆只相隔二十公尺遠，我卻還是沒看到任何東西。

　　小王子沉默一會兒後，又開口了：

　　「你的毒液夠毒嗎？你確定不會讓我痛苦太久吧？」

　　我停住腳步，內心感到一陣刺痛。但我仍然無法理解他在說什麼。

「你走吧。」小王子說，「我要下來了。」

我低頭看向牆腳，嚇了一跳。我看到一條豎起身面對小王子的黃蛇，牠三十秒內就能讓人致命。我從口袋裡掏出左輪手槍，奔跑過去。蛇一聽見聲響，便溜進沙堆裡，就像一條潺流的小溪慢慢地游移，並帶著一絲金屬般聲響，溜進石縫中。

我到達牆邊時，剛好及時抱住小王子——他的臉色蒼白得像一張紙。

「這是怎麼回事？你怎麼在和蛇說話？」

我解開他習慣圍住的金色圍巾，用一塊溼布擦擦他的太陽穴，又給他喝了一些水。我不敢再問他任何問題了。

他憂傷地看著我，雙手圍著我的脖子。我感覺得到他的心跳聲，就像一隻遭受槍傷，垂死鳥兒般的心跳聲……

「我很高興你終於解決引擎的問題了。」他說，「現在你可以回家了……」

「你怎麼知道？」

我就是來告訴他，我修理引擎的工作順利地讓我不敢置信。

他沒有回答我的問題，接著說：

「我今天也要回家了……」

又悲傷地說：

「路途好遠……也比較困難……」

我內心知道，不尋常的事就要發生了。我像抱著孩子，緊緊地將他擁入懷裡。他似乎快一頭掉進無底的深淵裡，而我卻無法拉住他……

　　他的表情非常嚴肅，遙遠而迷茫。

　　「我有你的羊，羊的盒子，還有口罩……」

　　然後，他哀傷地笑了。

　　我等待了很長一段時間，終於看到他的臉漸漸恢復紅潤。

　　「可憐的小傢伙，」我告訴他，「你很害怕……」

　　他真的很害怕，但他靜靜地笑了。

　　「今天晚上，我會更害怕……」

　　再一次，我的心，因為這種無力感而覺得寒冷。

　　我知道，我絕對無法忍受今後再也聽不見他的笑聲。對我來說，他的笑聲就像沙漠中的泉水。

　　「小人兒，」我說，「我想再繼續聽到你的笑聲。」

　　可是他卻說：

　　「今晚就滿一年了……我的星球會在我一年前降落地點的正上方……」

　　「小人兒，求求你告訴我，蛇、見面的地方、還有星星，都只是一場惡夢，對不對？」

　　但是他並沒有回答我的問題，他說：

　　「真正重要的東西——是看不見的……」

　　「對，我知道……」

「就像我的花一樣。如果你愛上了某個星球上的一朵花，那麼只要在夜晚仰望星空，就會覺得所有的星星都開出花朵……」

「沒錯……」

「就像水一樣。因為滑輪和繩子，使得你讓我喝的水有如音樂一般。你記得嗎？它是如此甜美。」

「是的……」

「你將會在夜晚仰望星空，找尋我的星球。我住的那顆星球太小，我沒辦法指出來給你看，不過這樣反而更好。對你而言，我的星球只是眾多星星中的其中一顆，所以你就會看著所有星星，他們都會變成你的朋友。而且，現在我還要給你一個禮物……」

然後，他又笑了。

「噢，小人兒，親愛的小人兒！我多麼喜歡聽到你的笑聲！」

「對啊，這笑聲就是我的禮物。它就會像我們喝的水一樣……」

「什麼意思？」

「星星對每個人的意義是不一樣的。對旅行的人來說，星星可以指引方向；對有些人來說，星星只是一些小光點；對專家來說，星星是研究對象；對我遇到的商人來說，星星是金錢。然而，所有的星星都是沉默的。只有你的星星顯得特別不同。」

「你的意思是？」

「我會住在這其中的一顆星星上面，在某一顆星星上微笑著，每當夜晚你仰望星空時，就會像是看到所有的星星在微笑一樣！」

於是他繼續笑了。

「當你撫平你的悲傷時（每個人都會克服的），你就會是我永遠的朋友，你要跟我一起笑。有時候，當你為了與我一同歡笑而打開窗戶時……你的朋友一定會因為你看著天空微笑，而感到驚訝。到時候你就可以告訴他們，『沒錯，星星常讓我笑了！』然後他們就會認為你瘋了。這是我給你的小小惡作劇……」

他再次笑了。

「這就像是我給你很多會笑的小鈴鐺，而不是小星星一樣……」

說完，他又笑了。然後他又變得嚴肅。

「聽著，今晚……不要來！」

「我不會留下你一個人的。」我說。

「我看起會很痛苦，而且一副快死掉的樣子。事情看起來會像那樣，所以我不要你來，也不要你看……不要來……」

「我不會丟下你一個人的。」

可是他開始擔心。

「我告訴你──這是因為蛇──你不能被牠咬到，蛇是壞東西，牠們咬你可能只是為了好玩而已……」

「我不會丟下你一個人的。」

突然間，他平靜下來：

「嗯！牠應該沒有足夠的毒液可以咬第二口……」

那天晚上，我沒有看到他出發，因為他一聲不響地走了。當我追上他時，他正迅速且堅定地向前走，他只是對我說：「噢！你來了……」

他握住我的手，看起來很憂心。

「你不該來的，你會很難過。看到我快死掉的樣子，即使那不是真的。」

我沉默不語。

「你知道的……路途太遙遠了，我不能帶著這副軀殼呀，那太重了……」

我沉默不語。

「那只是一副老舊的空殼而已，你沒有必要為老舊的空殼而哀傷……」

我仍然沉默。

他有些洩氣，不過他又試圖振作：

「這將會很美好。你知道，我也會看著星星啊。所有星星都將會是帶有生鏽滑輪的井；所有星星都會流出水來讓我喝……」

我依舊沉默。

「那會很有趣！你會擁有五百萬個小鈴鐺，我會擁有五百萬口井……」

接著他也沉默了，因為淚水布滿了他的臉……

「就是這裡，讓我自己走吧。」

他坐了下來，因為感到害怕，他又說：

「你知道的……我必須對我的花負責。她是如此脆弱！如此天真無邪！她只有那四根沒用的刺，可以保護自己，對抗外界……」

我也坐了下來，因為我再也站不住了。

「現在——就這樣了……」

他又遲疑了一會兒。然後站起身往前踏了一步，我卻沒辦法移動。一道黃色的閃光接近他的腳踝，有一陣子他待在原地不動。沒有尖叫，他像一顆枯樹般輕輕地倒下。因為沙地的關係，他倒下時一點聲音也沒有。

第 26 章

第 27 章

如今已過了六年……

我一直沒有告訴別人這個故事。我的同伴都很高興發現我還活著，我卻很難過，但也只是告訴他們：「我累了。」

現在，我的悲傷稍稍平息了，也就是說——還未完全平息。我確定，他是真的回到他的星球了。因為天亮時，我並沒有發現他的遺體。而他的身體其實並不怎麼重……在夜晚，我愛看星星，聽它們的聲音就像是聽見五億個小鈴鐺在響一樣……

不過，有一件極不尋常的事……當我幫小王子畫口罩時，我忘記畫口罩的鬆緊帶了。這樣他是永遠也無法把口罩套到羊的嘴上。所以我常常想：他的星球上發生了什麼事？也許羊真的已經把花吃掉了……

偶爾我會想：「當然不會！小王子每晚都把玫瑰花放在玻璃罩裡，而且他會小心翼翼地看著他的羊……」然後我就會覺得很快樂，而所有的星星也跟著溫柔的笑了。

有時我又會想：「只要疏忽一下，後果就會很嚴重！萬一有天他忘記幫花蓋上玻璃罩，或者不小心讓羊跑了出來……」於是，所有的小鈴鐺就變成了眼淚……

這是一個謎題：對於喜愛小王子的你們來說──在某個地方，沒有人知道的某個地方，會不會有一隻我們不知道的羊，吃掉一朵玫瑰……世界會不會因此變得不同？

抬頭仰望天空，問問你自己：羊是否已經吃掉那朵花了？然後，你就會看到世界萬物是如何地改變……

沒有大人會了解──這是件多麼重要的事！

對我來說，這是世界上最美麗，也最令人哀傷的景像。這幅畫和前一幅畫是完全相同的。我又畫了一次，只是為了讓你更了解而已。這就是小王子出現在地球上，消失的地方。

仔細地看這幅畫，如果有一天你到非洲旅行，就可以在沙漠中再次認出這裡。如果你剛好經過，請你不要匆匆走過，在這顆星星底下稍待一會兒。如果出現了一個愛笑的小人兒走向你，如果他有著一頭金髮，而且從不回答你的問題，你將會知道他是誰。假若你心地善良，就不要讓我活在悲慘之中！請立刻寫信告訴我，告訴我：他回來了。

Prologue

I ask the indulgence of the children who may read this book for dedicating it to a grownup. I have a serious reason: he is the best friend I have in the world. I have another reason: this grown-up understands everything, even books about children. I have a third reason: he lives in France where he is hungry and cold. He needs cheering up. If all these reasons are not enough, I will dedicate the book to the child from whom this grown-up grew. All grown-ups were once children—although few of them remember it. And so I correct my dedication:

To Leon Werth
when he was a little boy

Chapter 1

Once when I was six years old I saw a magnificent picture in a book, called True Stories from Nature, about the primeval forest. It was a picture of a boa constrictor in the

act of swallowing an animal. Here is a copy of the drawing.

In the book it said: "Boa constrictors swallow their prey whole, without chewing it. After that they are not able to move, and they sleep through the six months that they need for digestion."

I pondered deeply, then, over the adventures of the jungle. And after some work with a colored pencil I succeeded in making my first drawing. My Drawing Number One. It looked like this:

I showed my masterpiece to the grown ups, and asked them whether the drawing frightened them.

But they answered: "Frighten? Why should any one be frightened by a hat?"

My drawing was not a picture of a hat. It was a picture of a boa constrictor digesting an elephant. But since the grown ups were not able to understand it, I made another drawing: I drew the inside of the boa constrictor, so that the grown ups could see it clearly. They always need to have things explained. My Drawing Number Two looked like this:

The grown ups' response, this time, was to advise me to lay aside my drawings of boa constrictors, whether from the inside or the outside, and devote myself instead to geography, history, arithmetic and grammar. That is why, at the age of six, I gave up what might have been a magnificent career as a painter. I had been disheartened by the failure of my Drawing Number One and my Drawing Number Two. Grown ups never understand anything by themselves, and it is tiresome for children to be always and forever explaining things to them.

So then I chose another profession, and learned to pilot airplanes. I have flown a little over all parts of the world; and it is true that geography has been very useful to me. At a glance I can distinguish China from Arizona. If one gets lost in the night, such knowledge is valuable.

In the course of this life I have had a great many encounters with a great many people who have been concerned with matters of consequence. I have lived a great deal among grown ups. I have seen them intimately, close at hand. And that hasn't much improved my opinion of them.

Whenever I met one of them who seemed to me at all clear sighted, I tried the experiment of showing him my Drawing Number One, which I have always kept. I would try to find out, so, if this was a person of true understanding. But, whoever it was, he, or she, would always say:

"That is a hat." Then I would never talk to that person

about boa constrictors, or primeval forests, or stars. I would bring myself down to his level. I would talk to him about bridge, and golf, and politics, and neckties. And the grown-up would be greatly pleased to have met such a sensible man.

Chapter 2

So I lived my life alone, without anyone that I could really talk to, until I had an accident with my plane in the Desert of Sahara, six years ago. Something was broken in my engine. And as I had with me neither a mechanic nor any passengers, I set myself to attempt the difficult repairs all alone. It was a question of life or death for me: I had scarcely enough drinking water to last a week.

The first night, then, I went to sleep on the sand, a thousand miles from any human habitation. I was more isolated than a shipwrecked sailor on a raft in the middle of the ocean. Thus you can imagine my amazement, at sunrise, when I was awakened by an odd little voice. It said:

"If you please draw me a sheep!"

"What!"

"Draw me a sheep!"

I jumped to my feet, completely thunderstruck. I blinked my eyes hard. I looked carefully all around me. And I saw a most extraordinary small person, who stood there examining me with great seriousness. Here you may see the best potrait that, later, I was able to make of him. But my drawing is certainly very much less charming than its model.

That, however, is not my fault. The grown ups discouraged me in my painter's career when I was six years old, and I never learned to draw anything, except boas from the outside and boas from the inside.

Now I stared at this sudden apparition with my eyes fairly starting out of my head in astonishment. Remember, I had crashed in the desert a thousand miles from any inhabited region. And yet my little man seemed neither to be straying uncertainly among the sands, nor to be fainting from fatigue or hunger or thirst or fear.

Nothing about him gave any suggestion of a child lost in the middle of the desert, a thousand miles from any human habitation. When at last I was able to speak, I said to him:

"But what are you doing here?"

And in answer he repeated, very slowly, as if he were

speaking of a matter of great consequence: "If you please—draw me a sheep..."

When a mystery is too overpowering, one dare not disobey. Absurd as it might seem to me, a thousand miles from any human habitation and in danger of death, I took out of my pocket a sheet of paper and my fountain pen. But then I remembered how my studies had been concentrated on geography, history, arithmetic, and grammar, and I told the little chap (a little crossly, too) that I did not know how to draw. He answered me:

"That doesn't matter. Draw me a sheep..."

But I had never drawn a sheep. So I drew for him one of the two pictures I had drawn so often. It was that of the boa constrictor from the outside. And I was astounded to hear the little fellow greet it with, "No, no, no! I do not want an elephant inside a boa constrictor. A boa constrictor is a very dangerous creature, and an elephant is very cumbersome. Where I live, everything is very small. What I need is a sheep. Draw me a sheep."

So then I made a drawing.

He looked at it carefully, then he said:

"No. This sheep is already very sickly. Make me another."

So I made another drawing.

My friend smiled gently and indulgenty.

"You see yourself," he said, "that this is not a sheep. This is a ram. It has horns."

So then I did my drawing over once more.

But it was rejected too, just like the others.

"This one is too old. I want a sheep that will live a long time."

By this time my patience was exhausted, because I was in a hurry to start taking my engine apart. So I tossed off this drawing.

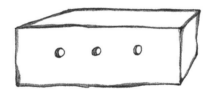

And I threw out an explanation with it.

"This is only his box. The sheep you asked for is inside."

I was very surprised to see a light break over the face of my young judge:

"That is exactly the way I wanted it! Do you think that this sheep will have to have a great deal of grass?"

"Why?"

"Because where I live everything is very small..."

"There will surely be enough grass for him," I said. "It is a very small sheep that I have given you."

He bent his head over the drawing:

"Not so small that Look! He has gone to sleep..." And that is how I made the acquaintance of the little prince.

Chapter 3

It took me a long time to learn where he came from. The little prince, who asked me so many questions, never seemed to hear the ones I asked him. It was from words dropped by chance that, little by little, everything was revealed to me.

The first time he saw my airplane, for instance (I shall not draw my airplane; that would be much too complicated for me), he asked me:

"What is that object?"

"That is not an object. It flies. It is an airplane. It is my airplane."

And I was proud to have him learn that I could fly.

He cried out, then:

"What! You dropped down from the sky?"

"Yes," I answered, modestly.

"Oh! That is funny!"

And the little prince broke into a lovely peal of laughter, which irritated me very much. I like my misfortunes to be taken seriously.

Then he added:

"So you, too, come from the sky! Which is your planet?"

At that moment I caught a gleam of light in the impenetrable mystery of his presence; and I demanded, abruptly:

"Do you come from another planet?"

But he did not reply. He tossed his head gently, without taking his eyes from my plane:

"It is true that on that you can't have come from very far away..."

And he sank into a reverie, which lasted a long time. Then, taking my sheep out of his pocket, he buried himself in the contemplation of his treasure.

You can imagine how my curiosity was aroused by this half-confidence about the "other planets." I made a great effort, therefore, to find out more on this subject.

"My little man, where do you come from? What is this 'where I live,' of which you speak? Where do you want to take your sheep?"

After a reflective silence he answered:

"The thing that is so good about the box you have given me is that at night he can use it as his house."

"That is so. And if you are good I will give you a string, too, so that you can tie him during the day, and a post to tie him to."

But the little prince seemed shocked by this offer:

"Tie him! What a queer idea!"

"But if you don't tie him," I said, "he will wander off somewhere, and get lost."

My friend broke into another peal of laughter:

"But where do you think he would go?"

"Anywhere. Straight ahead of him."

Then the little prince said, earnestly:

"That doesn't matter. Where I live, everything is so small!"

And, with perhaps a hint of sadness, he added:

"Straight ahead of him, nobody can go very far..."

Chapter 4

I had thus learned a second fact of great importance: this was that the planet the little prince came from was scarcely any larger than a house!

But that did not really surprise me much. I knew very well that in addition to the great planets such as the Earth, Jupiter, Mars, Venus to which we have given names, there are also hundreds of others, some of which are so small that one has a hard time seeing them through the telescope. When an astronomer discovers one of these he does not give it a name, but only a number. He might call it, for example, "Asteroid 325."

I have serious reason to believe that the planet from which the little prince came is the asteroid known as B612.

This asteroid has only once been seen

through the telescope. That was by a Turkish astronomer, in 1909. On making his discovery, the astronomer had presented it to the International Astronomical Congress, in a great demonstration. But he was in Turkish costume, and so nobody would believe what he said.

Grown ups are like that...

Fortunately, however, for the reputation of Asteroid B612, a Turkish dictator made a law that his subjects, under pain of death, should change to European costume. So in 1920 the astronomer gave his demonstration all over again, dressed with impressive style and elegance. And this time everybody accepted his report.

If I have told you these details about the asteroid, and made a note of its number for you, it is on account of the grown-ups and their ways. When you tell them that you have made a new friend, they never ask you any

questions about essential matters. They never say to you, "What does his voice sound like? What games does he love best? Does he collect butterflies?" Instead, they demand: "How old is he? How many brothers has he? How much does he weigh? How much money does his father make?" Only from these figures do they think they have learned anything about him.

If you were to say to the grown ups: "I saw a beautiful house made of rosy brick, with geraniums in the windows and doves on the roof," they would not be able to get any idea of that house at all. You would have to say to them: "I saw a house that cost $20,000." Then they would exclaim: "Oh, what a pretty house that is!"

Just so, you might say to them: "The proof that the little prince existed is that he was charming, that he laughed, and that he was looking for a sheep. If anybody wants a sheep, that is a proof that he exists." And what good would it do to tell them that? They would shrug their shoulders, and treat you like a child. But if you said to them: "The planet he came from is Asteroid B-612," then they would be convinced, and leave you in peace from their questions.

They are like that. One must not hold it against them. Children should always show great forbearance toward grown-up people.

But certainly, for us who understand life, figures are a matter of indifference. I should have liked to begin this story

in the fashion of the fairy-tales. I should have like to say: "Once upon a time there was a little prince who lived on a planet that was scarcely any bigger than himself, and who had need of a sheep..."

To those who understand life, that would have given a much greater air of truth to my story.

For I do not want any one to read my book carelessly. I have suffered too much grief in setting down these memories. Six years have already passed since my friend went away from me, with his sheep. If I try to describe him here, it is to make sure that I shall not forget him. To forget a friend is sad. Not every one has had a friend. And if I forget him, I may become like the grown-ups who are no longer interested in anything but figures...

It is for that purpose, again, that I have bought a box of paints and some pencils. It is hard to take up drawing again at my age, when I have never made any pictures except those of the boa constrictor from the outside and the boa constrictor from the inside, since I was six. I shall certainly try to make my portraits as true to life as possible. But I am not at all sure of success. One drawing goes along all right, and another has no resemblance to its subject. I make some errors, too, in the little prince's height: in one place he is too tall and in another too short. And I feel some doubts about the color of his costume. So I fumble along as best I can, now good, now bad, and I hope generally fair to middling.

In certain more important details I shall make mistakes, also. But that is something that will not be my fault. My friend never explained anything to me. He thought, perhaps, that I was like himself. But I, alas, do not know how to see sheep through the walls of boxes. Perhaps I am a little like the grown-ups. I have had to grow old.

Chapter 5

As each day passed I would learn, in our talk, something about the little prince's planet, his departure from it, his journey. The information would come very slowly, as it might chance to fall from his thoughts. It was in this way that I heard, on the third day, about the catastrophe of the baobabs.

This time, once more, I had the sheep to thank for it. For the little prince asked me abruptly as if seized by a grave doubt "It is true, isn't it, that sheep eat little bushes?"

"Yes, that is true."

"Ah! I am glad!"

I did not understand why it was so important that sheep should eat little bushes.

But the little prince added:

"Then it follows that they also eat baobabs?"

I pointed out to the little prince that baobabs were not little bushes, but, on the contrary, trees as big as castles; and that even if he took a whole herd of elephants away with him, the herd would not eat up one single baobab.

The idea of the herd of elephants made the little prince laugh.

"We would have to put them one on top of the other," he said.

But he made a wise comment:

"Before they grow so big, the baobabs start out by being little."

"That is strictly correct," I said. "But why do you want the sheep to eat the little baobabs?"

He answered me at once, "Oh, come, come!", as if he were speaking of something that was self-evident. And I was obliged to make a great mental effort to solve this problem, without any assistance.

Indeed, as I learned, there were on the planet where the little prince lived as on all planets good plants and bad plants. In consequence, there were good seeds from good plants, and bad seeds from bad plants. But seeds are invisible. They sleep deep in the heart of the earth's darkness, until someone among them is seized with the desire to awaken. Then this little seed will stretch itself and begin—timidly at first—to push a charming little sprig inoffensively upward toward the sun. If it is only a sprout of radish or the sprig of a rose-bush, one would let it grow wherever it might wish. But when it is a bad plant, one must destroy it as soon as possible, the very first instant that one recognizes it.

Now there were some terrible seeds on the planet that

was the home of the little prince; and these were the seeds of
the baobab. The soil of that planet was infested with them. A
baobab is something you will never, never be able to get rid
of if you attend to it too late. It spreads over the entire
planet. It bores clear through it with its roots. And if the
planet is too small, and the baobabs are too many, they split it
in pieces...

"It is a question of discipline," the little prince said to me later on. "When you've finished your own toilet in the morning, then it is time to attend to the toilet of your planet, just so, with the greatest care. You must see to it that you pull up regularly all the baobabs, at the very first moment when they can be distinguished from the rosebushes which they resemble so closely in their earliest youth. It is very tedious work," the little prince added, "but very easy."

And one day he said to me: "You ought to make a beautiful drawing, so that the children where you live can see exactly how all this is. That would be very useful to them if they were to travel some day. Sometimes," he added, "there is no harm in putting off a piece of work until another day. But when it is a matter of baobabs, that always means a catastrophe. I knew a planet that was inhabited by a lazy man. He neglected three little bushes..."

So, as the little prince described it to me, I have made a drawing of that planet. I do not much like to take the tone of a moralist. But the danger of the baobabs is so little understood, and such considerable risks would be run by anyone who might get lost on an asteroid, that for once I am breaking through my reserve.

"Children," I say plainly, "watch out for the baobabs!"

My friends, like myself, have been skirting this danger for a long time, without ever knowing it; and so it is for them that I have worked so hard over this drawing. The lesson which I pass on by this means is worth all the trouble it has cost me.

The Baobabs

Perhaps you will ask me, "Why are there no other drawing in this book as magnificent and impressive as this drawing of the baobabs?" The reply is simple. I have tried. But with the others I have not been successful. When I made the drawing of the baobabs I was carried beyond myself by the inspiring force of urgent necessity.

Chapter 6

Oh, little prince! Bit by bit I came to understand the secrets of your sad little life...

For a long time you had found your only entertainment in the quiet pleasure of looking at the sunset. I learned that new detail on the morning of the fourth day, when you said to me:

"I am very fond of sunsets. Come, let us go look at a sunset now."

"But we must wait," I said.

"Wait? For what?"

"For the sunset. We must wait until it is time."

At first you seemed to be very much surprised. And then you laughed to yourself.

You said to me:

"I am always thinking that I am at home!"

Just so. Everybody knows that when it is noon in the United States the sun is setting over France.

If you could fly to France in one minute, you could go straight into the sunset, right from noon. Unfortunately, France is too far away for that. But on your tiny planet, my little prince, all you need do is move your chair a few steps. You can see the day end and the twilight falling whenever you like...

"One day," you said to me, "I saw the sunset forty four times!"

And a little later you added:

"You know one loves the sunset, when one is so sad..."

"Were you so sad, then?" I asked, "on the day of the forty-four sunsets?"

But the little prince made no reply.

Chapter 7

On the fifth day again, as always, it was thanks to the sheep the secret of the little prince's life was revealed to me. Abruptly, without anything to lead up to it, and as if the question had been born of long and silent meditation on his problem, he demanded:

"A sheep if it eats little bushes, does it eat flowers, too?"

"A sheep," I answered, "eats anything it finds in its reach."

"Even flowers that have thorns?"

"Yes, even flowers that have thorns."

"Then the thorns—what use are they?"

I did not know. At that moment I was very busy trying to unscrew a bolt that had got stuck in my engine. I was very much worried, for it was becoming clear to me that the breakdown of my plane was extremely serious. And I had so little drinking-water left that I had to fear for the worst.

"The thorns what use are they?"

The little prince never let go of a question, once he had asked it. As for me, I was upset over that bolt. And I answered with the first thing that came into my head:

"The thorns are of no use at all. Flowers have thorns just for spite!"

"Oh!"

There was a moment of complete silence. Then the little prince flashed back at me, with a kind of resentfulness:

"I don't believe you! Flowers are weak creatures. They are naïve. They reassure themselves as best they can. They believe that their thorns are terrible weapons..."

I did not answer. At that instant I was saying to myself: "If this bolt still won't turn, I am going to knock it out with the hammer." Again the little prince disturbed my thoughts.

"And you actually believe that the flowers—"

"Oh, no!" I cried. "No, no no! I don't believe anything. I answered you with the first thing that came into my head. Don't you see I am very busy with matters of consequence!"

He stared at me, thunderstruck.

"Matters of consequence!"

He looked at me there, with my hammer in my hand, my fingers black with engine grease, bending down over an object which seemed to him extremely ugly...

"You talk just like the grown ups!"

That made me a little ashamed. But he went on, relentlessly:

"You mix everything up together... You confuse everything..."

He was really very angry. He tossed his golden curls in the breeze.

"I know a planet where there is a certain red faced gentleman. He has never smelled a flower. He has never looked at a star. He has never loved any one. He has never done anything in his life but add up figures. And all day he says over and over, just like you: 'I am busy with matters of consequence!' And that makes him swell up with pride. But he is not a man he is a mushroom!"

"A what?"

"A mushroom!"

The little prince was now white with rage.

"The flowers have been growing thorns for millions of years. For millions of years the sheep have been eating them just the same. And is it not a matter of consequence to try to understand why the flowers go to so much trouble to grow thorns which are never of any use to them? Is the warfare between the sheep and the flowers not important? Is this not of more consequence than a fat red-faced gentleman's sums? And if I know I, myself one flower which is unique in the world, which grows nowhere but on my planet, but which one little sheep can destroy in a single bite some morning, without even noticing what he is doing—

Oh! You think that is not important!"

His face turned from white to red as he continued:

"If some one loves a flower, of which just one single blossom grows in all the millions and millions of stars, it is enough to make him happy just to look at the stars. He can say to himself, 'Somewhere, my flower is there...' But if the sheep eats the flower, in one moment all his stars will be darkened... And you think that is not important!"

He could not say anything more. His words were choked by sobbing.

The night had fallen. I had let my tools drop from my hands. Of what moment now was my hammer, my bolt, or thirst, or death? On one star, one planet, my planet, the Earth, there was a little prince to be comforted. I took him in my arms, and rocked him. I said to him:

"The flower that you love is not in danger. I will draw you a muzzle for your sheep. I will draw you a railing to put around your flower. I will"

I did not know what to say to him. I felt awkward and blundering. I did not know how I could reach him, where I could overtake him and go on hand in hand with him once more.

It is such a secret place, the land of tears.

Chapter 8

I soon learned to know this flower better. On the little prince's planet the flowers had always been very simple. They had only one ring of petals; they took up no room at all; they were a trouble to nobody. One morning they would appear in the grass, and by night they would have faded peacefully away. But one day, from a seed blown from no one knew where, a new flower had come up; and the little prince had watched very closely over this small sprout which was not like any other small sprouts on his planet. It might, you see, have been a new kind of baobab.

The shrub soon stopped growing, and began to get ready to produce a flower. The little prince, who was present at the first appearance of a huge bud, felt at once that some sort of miraculous apparition must emerge from it. But the flower was not satisfied to complete the preparations for her beauty in the shelter of her green chamber. She chose her colours with the greatest care. She adjusted her petals one by one. She did not wish to go out into the world all rumpled, like the field poppies. It was only in the full radiance of her beauty that she wished to appear.

Oh, yes! She was a coquettish creature! And her mysterious adornment lasted for days and days.

Then one morning, exactly at sunrise, she suddenly showed herself.

And, after working with all this painstaking precision, she yawned and said:

"Ah! I am scarcely awake. I beg that you will excuse me. My petals are still all disarranged..."

But the little prince could not restrain his admiration:

"Oh! How beautiful you are!"

"Am I not?" the flower responded, sweetly. "And I was born at the same moment as the sun..."

The little prince could guess easily enough that she was not any too modest—but how moving and exciting she was!

"I think it is time for breakfast," she added an instant later. "If you would have the kindness to think of my needs"

And the little prince, completely abashed, went to look for a sprinkling-can of fresh water. So, he tended the flower.

So, too, she began very quickly to torment him with her vanity which was, if the truth be known, a little difficult to

deal with. One day, for instance, when she was speaking of her four thorns, she said to the little prince:

"Let the tigers come with their claws!"

"There are no tigers on my planet," the little prince objected. "And, anyway, tigers do not eat weeds."

"I am not a weed," the flower replied, sweetly.

"Please excuse me..."

"I am not at all afraid of tigers," she went on, "but I have a horror of drafts. I suppose you wouldn't have a screen for me?"

"A horror of drafts that is bad luck, for a plant," remarked the little prince, and added to himself, "This flower is a very complex creature..."

"At night I want you to put me under a glass globe. It is very cold where you live. In the place I came from..."

But she interrupted herself at that point. She had come in the form of a seed. She could not have known anything of any other worlds. Embarassed over having let herself be caught on the verge of such a naïve untruth, she coughed two or three times, in order to put the little prince in the wrong.

"The screen?"

"I was just going to look for it when you spoke to me..."

Then she forced her cough a little more so that he should suffer from remorse just the same.

So the little prince, in spite of all the good will that was inseparable from his love, had soon come to doubt her. He had taken seriously words which were without importance, and it made him very unhappy.

"I ought not to have listened to her," he confided to me one day. "One never ought to listen to the flowers. One should simply look at them and breathe their fragrance. Mine perfumed all my planet. But I did not know how to take pleasure in all her

grace. This tale of claws, which disturbed me so much, should only have filled my heart with tenderness and pity."

And he continued his confidences:

"The fact is that I did not know how to understand anything! I ought to have judged by deeds and not by words. She cast her fragrance and her radiance over me. I ought never to have run away from her... I ought to have guessed all the affection that lay behind her poor little strategems. Flowers are so inconsistent!

But I was too young to know how to love her..."

Chapter 9

I believe that for his escape he took advantage of the migration of a flock of wild birds. On the morning of his departure he put his planet in perfect order. He carefully cleaned out his active volcanoes. He possessed two active volcanoes; and they were very convenient for heating his breakfast in the morning. He also had one volcano that was extinct. But, as he said, "One never knows!" So he cleaned out the extinct volcano, too. If they are well cleaned out, volcanoes burn slowly and steadily, without any eruptions. Volcanic eruptions are like fires in a chimney.

On our earth we are obviously much too small to clean out our volcanoes. That is why they bring no end of trouble upon us.

The little prince also pulled up, with a certain sense of dejection, the last little shoots of the baobabs. He believed that he would never want to return. But on this last morning all these familiar tasks seemed very precious to him. And when he watered the flower for the last time, and prepared to place her under the

shelter of her glass globe, he realised that he was very close to tears.

"Goodbye," he said to the flower.

But she made no answer.

"Goodbye," he said again.

The flower coughed. But it was not because she had a cold.

"I have been silly," she said to him, at last. "I ask your forgiveness. Try to be happy..."

He was surprised by this absence of reproaches. He stood there all bewildered, the glass globe held arrested in mid air. He did not understand this quiet sweetness.

"Of course I love you," the flower said to him. "It is my fault that you have not known it all the while. That is of no importance. But you you have been just as foolish as I. Try to be happy... let the glass globe be. I don't want it any more."

"But the wind"

"My cold is not so bad as all that... the cool night air will do me good. I am a flower."

"But the animals"

"Well, I must endure the presence of two or three caterpillars if I wish to become acquainted with the butterflies. It seems that they are very beautiful. And if not the butterflies and the caterpillars who will call upon me? You will be far away... as for the large animals I am not at all afraid of any of them. I have my claws."

And, naïvely, she showed her four thorns. Then she added:

"Don't linger like this. You have decided to go away. Now go!"

For she did not want him to see her crying. She was such a proud flower...

Chapter 10

He found himself in the neighborhood of the asteroids 325, 326, 327, 328, 329, and 330. He began, therefore, by visiting them, in order to add to his knowledge.

The first of them was inhabited by a king. Clad in royal purple and ermine, he was seated upon a throne which was at the same time both simple and majestic.

"Ah! Here is a subject," exclaimed the king, when he saw the little prince coming.

And the little prince asked himself:

"How could he recognize me when he had never seen me before?"

He did not know how the world is simplified for kings. To them, all men are subjects.

"Approach, so that I may see you better," said the king, who felt consumingly proud of being at last a king over somebody.

The little prince looked everywhere to find a place to sit down; but the entire planet was crammed and obstructed by the

king's magnificent ermine robe. So he remained standing upright, and, since he was tired, he yawned.

"It is contrary to etiquette to yawn in the presence of a king," the monarch said to him. "I forbid you to do so."

"I can't help it. I can't stop myself," replied the little prince, thoroughly embarrassed. "I have come on a long journey, and I have had no sleep..."

"Ah, then," the king said. "I order you to yawn. It is years since I have seen anyone yawning. Yawns, to me, are objects of curiosity. Come, now! Yawn again! It is an order."

"That frightens me... I cannot, any more..." murmured the little prince, now completely abashed.

"Hum! Hum!" replied the king. "Then I order you sometimes to yawn and sometimes to " He sputtered a little, and seemed vexed.

For what the king fundamentally insisted upon was that his authority should be respected. He tolerated no disobedience. He was an absolute monarch. But, because he was a very good man, he made his orders reasonable.

"If I ordered a general," he would say, by way of example, "if I ordered a general to change himself into a sea bird, and if the general did not obey me, that would not be the fault of the general. It would be my fault."

"May I sit down?" came now a timid inquiry from the little prince.

"I order you to do so," the king answered him, and

majestically gathered in a fold of his ermine mantle.

But the little prince was wondering... The planet was tiny. Over what could this king really rule?

"Sire," he said to him, "I beg that you will excuse my asking you a question—"

"I order you to ask me a question," the king hastened to assure him.

"Sire over what do you rule?"

"Over everything," said the king, with magnificent simplicity.

"Over everything?"

The king made a gesture, which took in his planet, the other planets, and all the stars.

"Over all that?" asked the little prince.

"Over all that," the king answered.

For his rule was not only absolute: it was also universal.

"And the stars obey you?"

"Certainly they do," the king said. "They obey instantly. I do not permit insubordination."

Such power was a thing for the little prince to marvel at. If he had been master of such complete authority, he would have been able to watch the sunset, not forty-four times in one day, but seventy-two, or even a hundred, or even two hundred times, with out ever having to move his chair. And because he felt a bit sad as he remembered his little planet which he had forsaken, he plucked up his courage to ask the king a favor:

"I should like to see a sunset... do me that kindness... Order

the sun to set..."

"If I ordered a general to fly from one flower to another like a butterfly, or to write a tragic drama, or to change himself into a sea bird, and if the general did not carry out the order that he had received, which one of us would be in the wrong?" the king demanded. "The general, or myself?"

"You," said the little prince firmly.

"Exactly. One much require from each one the duty which each one can perform," the king went on. "Accepted authority rests first of all on reason. If you ordered your people to go and throw themselves into the sea, they would rise up in revolution. I have the right to require obedience because my orders are reasonable."

"Then my sunset?" the little prince reminded him: for he never forgot a question once he had asked it.

"You shall have your sunset. I shall command it. But, according to my science of government, I shall wait until conditions are favorable."

"When will that be?" inquired the little prince.

"Hum! Hum!" replied the king; and before saying anything else he consulted a bulky almanac. "Hum! Hum! That will be about about that will be this evening about twenty minutes to eight. And you will see how well I am obeyed."

The little prince yawned. He was regretting his lost sunset. And then, too, he was already beginning to be a little bored.

"I have nothing more to do here," he said to the king. "So I

shall set out on my way again."

"Do not go," said the king, who was very proud of having a subject. "Do not go. I will make you a Minister!"

"Minister of what?"

"Minster of Justice!"

"But there is nobody here to judge!"

"We do not know that," the king said to him. "I have not yet made a complete tour of my kingdom. I am very old. There is no room here for a carriage. And it tires me to walk."

"Oh, but I have looked already!" said the little prince, turning around to give one more glance to the other side of the planet. On that side, as on this, there was nobody at all...

"Then you shall judge yourself," the king answered. "that is the most difficult thing of all. It is much more difficult to judge oneself than to judge others. If you succeed in judging yourself rightly, then you are indeed a man of true wisdom."

"Yes," said the little prince, "but I can judge myself anywhere. I do not need to live on this planet.

"Hum! Hum!" said the king. "I have good reason to believe that somewhere on my planet there is an old rat. I hear him at night. You can judge this old rat. From time to time you will condemn him to death. Thus his life will depend on your justice.

But you will pardon him on each occasion; for he must be treated thriftily. He is the only one we have."

"I," replied the little prince, "do not like to condemn anyone to death. And now I think I will go on my way."

"No," said the king.

But the little prince, having now completed his preparations for departure, had no wish to grieve the old monarch.

"If Your Majesty wishes to be promptly obeyed," he said, "he should be able to give me a reasonable order. He should be able, for example, to order me to be gone by the end of one minute. It seems to me that conditions are favorable..."

As the king made no answer, the little prince hesitated a moment. Then, with a sigh, he took his leave.

"I made you my Ambassador," the king called out, hastily.

He had a magnificent air of authority.

"The grown ups are very strange," the little prince said to himself, as he continued on his journey.

Chapter 11

The second planet was inhabited by a conceited man.

"Ah! Ah! I am about to receive a visit from an admirer!" he exclaimed from afar, when he first saw the little prince coming.

For, to conceited men, all other men are admirers.

"Good morning," said the little prince. "That is a queer hat you are wearing."

"It is a hat for salutes," the conceited man replied. "It is to raise in salute when people acclaim me. Unfortunately, nobody at all ever passes this way."

"Yes?" said the little prince, who did not understand what the conceited man was talking about.

"Clap your hands, one against the other," the conceited man now directed him.

The little prince clapped his hands. The conceited man raised his hat in a modest salute.

"This is more entertaining than the visit to the king," the little prince said to himself. And he began again to clap his hands, one against the other. The conceited man against raised his hat in salute.

After five minutes of this exercise the little prince grew tired of the game's monotony.

"And what should one do to make the hat come down?" he asked.

But the conceited man did not hear him. Conceited people never hear anything but praise.

"Do you really admire me very much?" he demanded of the little prince.

"What does that mean 'admire'?"

"To admire mean that you regard me as the handsomest, the best-dressed, the richest, and the most intelligent man on this planet."

"But you are the only man on your planet!"

"Do me this kindness. Admire me just the same."

"I admire you," said the little prince, shrugging his shoulders slightly, "but what is there in that to interest you so much?"

And the little prince went away.

"The grown-ups are certainly very odd," he said to himself, as he continued on his journey.

Chapter 12

The next planet was inhabited by a tippler. This was a very short visit, but it plunged the little prince into deep dejection.

"What are you doing there?" he said to the tippler, whom he found settled down in silence before a collection of empty bottles and also a collection of full bottles.

"I am drinking," replied the tippler, with a lugubrious air.

"Why are you drinking?" demanded the little prince.

"So that I may forget," replied the tippler.

"Forget what?" inquired the little prince, who already was sorry for him.

"Forget that I am ashamed," the tippler confessed, hanging his head.

"Ashamed of what?" insisted the little prince, who wanted to help him.

"Ashamed of drinking!" The tippler brought his speech to an end, and shut himself up in an impregnable silence.

And the little prince went away, puzzled.

"The grown-ups are certainly very, very odd," he said to himself, as he continued on his journey.

Chapter 13

The fourth planet belonged to a businessman. This man was so much occupied that he did not even raise his head at the little prince's arrival.

"Good morning," the little prince said to him. "Your cigarette has gone out."

"Three and two make five. Five and seven make twelve. Twelve and three make fifteen. Good morning. Fifteen and seven make twenty-two. Twenty-two and six make twenty-eight. I haven't time to light it again. Twenty-six and five make thirty-one. Phew! Then that makes five-hundred-and-one million, six-hundred-twenty-two-thousand, seven-hundred-thirty-one."

"Five hundred million what?" asked the little prince.

"Eh? Are you still there? Five-hundred and one million—I can't stop... I have so much to do! I am concerned with matters of consequence. I don't amuse myself with balderdash. Two and five make seven..."

"Five-hundred-and-one million what?" repeated the little

prince, who never in his life had let go of a question once he had asked it.

The businessman raised his head.

"During the fifty-four years that I have inhabited this planet, I have been disturbed only three times. The first time was twenty-two years ago, when some giddy goose fell from goodness knows where. He made the most frightful noise that resounded all over the place, and I made four mistakes in my addition. The second time, eleven years ago, I was disturbed by an attack of rheumatism. I don't get enough exercise. I have no time for loafing. The third time—well, this is it! I was saying, then, five -hundred-and-one millions—"

"Millions of what?"

The businessman suddenly realized that there was no hope of being left in peace until he answered this question.

"Millions of those little objects," he said, "which one sometimes sees in the sky."

"Flies?"

"Oh, no. Little glittering objects."

"Bees?"

"Oh, no. Little golden objects that set lazy men to idle dreaming. As for me, I am concerned with matters of consequence. There is no time for idle dreaming in my life."

"Ah! You mean the stars?"

"Yes, that's it. The stars."

"And what do you do with five-hundred millions of stars?"

"Five-hundred-and-one million, six-hundred-twenty-two

thousand, seven-hundred-thirty-one. I am concerned with matters of consequence: I am accurate."

"And what do you do with these stars?"

"What do I do with them?"

"Yes."

"Nothing. I own them."

"You own the stars?"

"Yes."

"But I have already seen a king who—"

"Kings do not own, they reign over. It is a very different matter."

"And what good does it do you to own the stars?"

"It does me the good of making me rich."

"And what good does it do you to be rich?"

"It makes it possible for me to buy more stars, if any are ever discovered."

"This man," the little prince said to himself, "reasons a little like my poor tippler..."

Nevertheless, he still had some more questions.

"How is it possible for one to own the stars?"

"To whom do they belong?" the businessman retorted, peevishly.

"I don't know. To nobody."

"Then they belong to me, because I was the first person to think of it."

"Is that all that is necessary?"

"Certainly. When you find a diamond that belongs to nobody, it is yours. When you discover an island that belongs to nobody, it is yours. When you get an idea before any one else, you take out a patent on it: it is yours. So with me: I own the stars, because nobody else before me ever thought of owning them."

"Yes, that is true," said the little prince. "And what do you do with them?"

"I administer them," replied the businessman. "I count them and recount them. It is difficult. But I am a man who is naturally interested in matters of consequence."

The little prince was still not satisfied.

"If I owned a silk scarf," he said, "I could put it around my neck and take it away with me. If I owned a flower, I could pluck that flower and take it away with me.

But you cannot pluck the stars from heaven..."

"No. But I can put them in the bank."

"Whatever does that mean?"

"That means that I write the number of my stars on a little paper. And then I put this paper in a drawer and lock it with a key."

"And that is all?"

"That is enough," said the businessman.

"It is entertaining," thought the little prince. "It is rather poetic. But it is of no great consequence."

On matters of consequence, the little prince had ideas which were very different from those of the grown-ups.

"I myself own a flower," he continued his conversation with the businessman, "which I water every day. I own three volcanoes, which I clean out every week (for I also clean out the one that is extinct; one never knows). It is of some use to my volcanoes, and it is of some use to my flower, that I own them. But you are of no use to the stars..."

The businessman opened his mouth, but he found nothing to say in answer. And the little prince went away.

"The grown-ups are certainly altogether extraordinary," he said simply, talking to himself as he continued on his journey.

Chapter 14

The fifth planet was very strange. It was the smallest of all. There was just enough room on it for a street lamp and a lamplighter. The little prince was not able to reach any explanation of the use of a street lamp and a lamplighter, somewhere in the heavens, on a planet which had no people, and not one house. But he said to himself, nevertheless:

"It may well be that this man is absurd. But he is not so absurd as the king, the conceited man, the businessman, and the tippler. For at least his work has some meaning. When he lights his street lamp, it is as if he brought one more star to life, or one flower. When he puts out his lamp, he sends the flower, or the star, to sleep.

That is a beautiful occupation. And since it is beautiful, it is truly useful."

When he arrived on the planet he respectfully saluted the lamplighter.

"Good morning. Why have you just put out your lamp?"

"Those are the orders," replied the lamplighter. "Good morning."

"What are the orders?"

"The orders are that I put out my lamp. Good evening."

And he lighted his lamp again.

"But why have you just lighted it again?"

"Those are the orders," replied the lamplighter.

"I do not understand," said the little prince.

"There is nothing to understand," said the lamplighter. "Orders are orders. Good morning."

And he put out his lamp.

Then he mopped his forehead with a handkerchief decorated with red squares.

"I follow a terrible profession. In the old days it was reasonable. I put the lamp out in the morning, and in the evening I lighted it again. I had the rest of the day for relaxation and the rest of the night for sleep."

"And the orders have been changed since that time?"

"The orders have not been changed," said the lamplighter. "That is the tragedy! From year to year the planet has turned more rapidly and the orders have not been changed!"

"Then what?" asked the little prince.

"Then—the planet now makes a complete turn every minute, and I no longer have a single second for repose. Once every minute I have to light my lamp and put it out!"

"That is very funny! A day lasts only one minute, here where

you live!"

"It is not funny at all!" said the lamplighter. "While we have been talking together a month has gone by."

"A month?"

"Yes, a month. Thirty minutes. Thirty days. Good evening."

And he lighted his lamp again.

As the little prince watched him, he felt that he loved this lamplighter who was so faithful to his orders. He remembered the sunsets which he himself had gone to seek, in other days, merely by pulling up his chair; and he wanted to help his friend.

"You know," he said, "I can tell you a way you can rest whenever you want to..."

"I always want to rest," said the lamplighter.

For it is possible for a man to be faithful and lazy at the same time.

The little prince went on with his explanation:

"Your planet is so small that three strides will take you all the way around it. To be always in the sunshine, you need only walk along rather slowly. When you want to rest, you will walk—and the day will last as long as you like."

"That doesn't do me much good," said the lamplighter. "The one thing I love in life is to sleep."

"Then you're unlucky," said the little prince.

"I am unlucky," said the lamplighter. "Good morning."

And he put out his lamp.

"That man," said the little prince to himself, as he continued farther on his journey, "that man would be scorned by all the others: by the king, by the conceited man, by the tippler, by the businessman. Nevertheless he is the only one of them all who does not seem to me ridiculous. Perhaps that is because he is thinking of something else besides himself."

He breathed a sigh of regret, and said to himself, again:

"That man is the only one of them all whom I could have made my friend. But his planet is indeed too small. There is no room on it for two people..."

What the little prince did not dare confess was that he was sorry most of all to leave this planet, because it was blest every day with 1440 sunsets!

Chapter 15

The sixth planet was ten times larger than the last one. It was inhabited by an old gentleman who wrote voluminous books.

"Oh, look! Here is an explorer!" he exclaimed to himself when he saw the little prince coming.

The little prince sat down on the table and panted a little. He had already traveled so much and so far!

"Where do you come from?" the old gentleman said to him.

"What is that big book?" said the little prince. "What are you doing?"

"I am a geographer," the old gentleman said to him.

"What is a geographer?" asked the little prince.

"A geographer is a scholar who knows the location of all the seas, rivers, towns, mountains, and deserts."

"That is very interesting," said the little prince. "Here at last is a man who has a real profession!" And he cast a look around him at the planet of the geographer. It was the most magnificent and stately planet that he had ever seen.

"Your planet is very beautiful," he said. "Has it any oceans?"

"I couldn't tell you," said the geographer.

"Ah!" The little prince was disappointed. "Has it any mountains?"

"I couldn't tell you," said the geographer.

"And towns, and rivers, and deserts?"

"I couldn't tell you that, either."

"But you are a geographer!"

"Exactly," the geographer said. "But I am not an explorer. I haven't a single explorer on my planet. It is not the geographer who goes out to count the towns, the rivers, the mountains, the seas, the oceans, and the deserts. The geographer is much too important to go loafing about. He does not leave his desk. But he receives the explorers in his study. He asks them questions, and he notes down what they recall of their travels. And if the recollections of any one among them seem interesting to him, the geographer orders an inquiry into that explorer's moral character."

"Why is that?"

"Because an explorer who told lies would bring disaster on the books of the

geographer. So would an explorer who drank too much."

"Why is that?" asked the little prince.

"Because intoxicated men see double. Then the geographer would note down two mountains in a place where there was only one."

"I know some one," said the little prince, "who would make a bad explorer."

"That is possible. Then, when the moral character of the explorer is shown to be good, an inquiry is ordered into his discovery."

"One goes to see it?"

"No. That would be too complicated. But one requires the explorer to furnish proofs. For example, if the discovery in question is that of a large mountain, one requires that large stones be brought back from it."

The geographer was suddenly stirred to excitement.

"But you—you come from far away! You are an explorer! You shall describe your planet to me!"

And, having opened his big register, the geographer sharpened his pencil. The recitals of explorers are put down first in pencil. One waits until the explorer has furnished proofs, before putting them down in ink.

"Well?" said the geographer expectantly.

"Oh, where I live," said the little prince, "it is not very interesting. It is all so small. I have three volcanoes. Two volcanoes are active and the other is extinct.

But one never knows."

"One never knows," said the geographer.

"I have also a flower."

"We do not record flowers," said the geographer.

"Why is that? The flower is the most beautiful thing on my planet!"

"We do not record them," said the geographer, "because they are ephemeral."

"What does that mean—'ephemeral'?"

"Geographies," said the geographer, "are the books which, of all books, are most concerned with matters of consequence. They never become old-fashioned. It is very rarely that a mountain changes its position. It is very rarely that an ocean empties itself of its waters. We write of eternal things."

"But extinct volcanoes may come to life again," the little prince interrupted.

"What does that mean—'ephemeral'?"

"Whether volcanoes are extinct or alive, it comes to the same thing for us," said the geographer. "The thing that matters to us is the mountain. It does not change."

"But what does that mean—'ephemeral'?" repeated the little prince, who never in his life had let go of a question, once he had asked it.

"It means, 'which is in danger of speedy disappearance.'"

"Is my flower in danger of speedy disappearance?"

"Certainly it is."

"My flower is ephemeral," the little prince said to himself, "and she has only four thorns to defend herself against the world. And I have left her on my planet, all alone!"

That was his first moment of regret. But he took courage once more.

"What place would you advise me to visit now?" he asked.

"The planet Earth," replied the geographer. "It has a good reputation."

And the little prince went away, thinking of his flower.

Chapter 16

So then the seventh planet was the Earth.

The Earth is not just an ordinary planet! One can count, there 111 kings (not forgetting, to be sure, the Negro kings among them), 7000 geographers, 900,000 businessmen, 7,500,000 tipplers, 311,000,000 conceited men—that is to say, about 2,000,000,000 grown-ups.

To give you an idea of the size of the Earth, I will tell you that before the invention of electricity it was necessary to maintain, over the whole of the six continents, a veritable army of 462,511 lamplighters for the street lamps.

Seen from a slight distance, that would make a splendid spectacle. The movements of this army would be regulated like those of the ballet in the opera.

First would come the turn of the lamplighters of New Zealand and Australia.

Having set their lamps alight, these would go off to sleep. Next, the lamplighters of China and Siberia would enter for their steps in the dance, and then they too would be waved back into the wings. After that would come the turn of the lamplighters of Russia and the Indies; then those of Africa and Europe, then those of South America; then those of South America; then those of North America.

And never would they make a mistake in the order of their entry upon the stage. It would be magnificent.

Only the man who was in charge of the single lamp at the North Pole, and his colleague who was responsible for the single lamp at the South Pole—only these two would live free from toil and care: they would be busy twice a year.

Chapter 17

When one wishes to play the wit, he sometimes wanders a little from the truth. I have not been altogether honest in what I have told you about the lamplighters.

And I realize that I run the risk of giving a false idea of our planet to those who do not k now it. Men occupy a very small place upon the Earth. If the two billion inhabitants who people its surface were all to stand upright and somewhat crowded together, as they do for some big public assembly, they could easily be put into one public square twenty miles long and twenty miles wide. All humanity could be piled up on a small Pacific islet.

The grown-ups, to be sure, will not believe you when you tell them that. They imagine that they fill a great deal of space. They fancy themselves as important as the baobabs. You should advise them, then, to make their own calculations. They adore fig ures, and that will please them. But do not waste your time on this extra task. It is unnecessary. You have,

I know, confidence in me.

When the little prince arrived on the Earth, he was very much surprised not to see any people. He was beginning to be afraid he had come to the wrong planet, when a coil of gold, the color of the moonlight, flashed across the sand.

"Good evening," said the little prince courteously.

"Good evening," said the snake.

"What planet is this on which I have come down?" asked the little prince.

"This is the Earth; this is Africa," the snake answered.

"Ah! Then there are no people on the Earth?"

"This is the desert. There are no people in the desert. The Earth is large," said the snake.

The little prince sat down on a stone, and raised his eyes toward the sky.

"I wonder," he said, "whether the stars are set alight in heaven so that one day each one of us may find his own again... Look at my planet. It is right there above us. But how far away it is!"

"It is beautiful," the snake said. "What has brought you here?"

"I have been having some trouble with a flower," said the little prince.

"Ah!" said the snake.

And they were both silent.

"Where are the men?" the little prince at last took up the conversation again. "It is a little lonely in the desert..."

"It is also lonely among men," the snake said.

The little prince gazed at him for a long time.

"You are a funny animal," he said at last. "You are no thicker than a finger..."

"But I am more powerful than the finger of a king," said the snake.

The little prince smiled.

"You are not very powerful. You haven't even any feet. You cannot even travel..."

"I can carry you farther than any ship could take you," said the snake.

He twined himself around the little prince's ankle, like a golden bracelet.

"Whomever I touch, I send back to the earth from whence he came," the snake spoke again. "But you are innocent and true, and you come from a star..."

The little prince made no reply.

"You move me to pity—you are so weak on this Earth

made of granite," the snake said. "I can help you, some day, if you grow too homesick for your own planet. I can—"

"Oh! I understand you very well," said the little prince. "But why do you always speak in riddles?"

"I solve them all," said the snake.

And they were both silent.

Chapter 18

The little prince crossed the desert and met with only one flower. It was a flower with three petals, a flower of no account at all.

"Good morning," said the little prince.

"Good morning," said the flower.

"Where are the men?" the little prince asked, politely.

The flower had once seen a caravan passing.

"Men?" she echoed. "I think there are six or seven of them in existence. I saw them, several years ago. But one never knows where to find them. The wind blows them away. They have no roots, and that makes their life very difficult."

"Goodbye," said the little prince.

"Goodbye," said the flower.

Chapter 19

After that, the little prince climbed a high mountain. The only mountains he had ever known were the three volcanoes, which came up to his knees. And he used the extinct volcano as a footstool. "From a mountain as high as this one," he said to himself, "I shall be able to see the whole planet at one glance, and all the people..."

But he saw nothing, save peaks of rock that were sharpened like needles.

"Good morning," he said courteously.

"Good morning—Good morning—Good morning," answered the echo.

"Who are you?" said the little prince.

"Who are you—Who are you—Who are you?" answered the echo.

"Be my friends. I am all alone," he said.

"I am all alone—all alone—all alone," answered the echo.

"What a queer planet!" he thought. "It is altogether dry,

and altogether pointed, and altogether harsh and forbidding. And the people have no imagination. They repeat whatever one says to them... On my planet I had a flower; she always was the first to speak..."

Chapter 20

But it happened that after walking for a long time through sand, and rocks, and snow, the little prince at last came upon a road. And all roads lead to the abodes of men.

"Good morning," he said.

He was standing before a garden, all a-bloom with roses.

"Good morning," said the roses.

The little prince gazed at them. They all looked like his flower.

"Who are you?" he demanded, thunderstruck.

"We are roses," the roses said.

And he was overcome with sadness. His flower had told him that she was the only one of her kind in all the universe. And here were five thousand of them, all alike, in one single garden!

"She would be very much annoyed," he said to himself, "if she should see that... she would cough most dreadfully, and she would pretend that she was dying, to avoid being laughed at. And I should be obliged to pretend that I was nursing her back to life—for if I did not do that, to humble myself also, she would really allow herself to die..."

Then he went on with his reflections: "I thought that I was rich, with a flower that was unique in all the world; and all I had was a common rose. A common rose, and three volcanoes that come up to my knees—and one of them perhaps extinct forever... that doesn't make me a very great prince..."

And he lay down in the grass and cried.

Chapter 21

It was then that the fox appeared.

"Good morning," said the fox.

"Good morning," the little prince responded politely, although when he turned around he saw nothing.

"I am right here," the voice said, "under the apple tree."

"Who are you?" asked the little prince, and added, "You are very pretty to look at."

"I am a fox," said the fox.

"Come and play with me," proposed the little prince. "I am so unhappy."

"I cannot play with you," the fox said. "I am not tamed."

"Ah! Please excuse me," said the little prince.

But, after some thought, he added:

"What does that mean—'tame'?"

"You do not live here," said the fox. "What is it that you are looking for?"

"I am looking for men," said the little prince. "What does

that mean—'tame'?"

"Men," said the fox. "They have guns, and they hunt. It is very disturbing. They also raise chickens. These are their only interests. Are you looking for chickens?"

"No," said the little prince. "I am looking for friends. What does that mean—'tame'?"

"It is an act too often neglected," said the fox. It means to establish ties."

"'To establish ties'?"

"Just that," said the fox. "To me, you are still nothing more than a little boy who is just like a hundred thousand other little boys. And I have no need of you. And you, on your part, have no need of me. To you, I am nothing more than a fox like a hundred thousand other foxes. But if you tame me, then we shall need each other. To me, you will be unique in all the world. To you, I shall be unique in all the world..."

"I am beginning to understand," said the little prince. "There is a flower... I think that she has tamed me..."

"It is possible," said the fox. "On the Earth one sees

all sorts of things."

"Oh, but this is not on the Earth!" said the little prince.

The fox seemed perplexed, and very curious.

"On another planet?"

"Yes."

"Are there hunters on this planet?"

"No."

"Ah, that is interesting! Are there chickens?"

"No."

"Nothing is perfect," sighed the fox.

But he came back to his idea.

"My life is very monotonous," the fox said. "I hunt chickens; men hunt me. All the chickens are just alike, and all the men are just alike. And, in consequence, I am a little bored. But if you tame me, it will be as if the sun came to shine on my life. I shall know the sound of a step that will be different from all the others. Other steps send me hurrying back underneath the ground. Yours will call me, like music, out of my burrow. And then look: you see the grain-fields down yonder? I do not ea t bread. Wheat is of no use to me. The wheat fields have nothing to say to me. And that is sad. But you have hair that is the colour of gold. Think how wonderful that will be when you have tamed me! The grain, which is also golden, will bring me bac k the thought of you. And I shall love to listen to the wind in the wheat..."

The fox gazed at the little prince, for a long time.

"Please—tame me!" he said.

"I want to, very much," the little prince replied. "But I have not much time. I have friends to discover, and a great many things to understand."

"One only understands the things that one tames," said the fox. "Men have no more time to understand anything. They buy things all ready made at the shops.

But there is no shop anywhere where one can buy friendship, and so men have no friends any more. If you want a friend, tame me..."

"What must I do, to tame you?" asked the little prince.

"You must be very patient," replied the fox. "First you will sit down at a little distance from me—like that—in the grass. I shall look at you out of the corner of my eye, and you will say nothing. Words are the source of misunderstandings.

But yo u will sit a little closer to me, every day..."

The next day the little prince came back.

"It would have been better to come back at the same hour," said the fox. "If, for example, you come at four o'clock in the afternoon, then at three o'clock I shall begin to be happy. I shall feel happier and happier as the hour advances. At four o'clock, I shall already be worrying and jumping about. I shall show you how happy I am! But if you come at just any time, I shall never know at what hour my heart is to be ready to greet you... One must observe the proper rites..."

"What is a rite?" asked the little prince.

"Those also are actions too often neglected," said the fox. "They are what make one day different from other days, one hour from other hours. There is a rite, for example, among my hunters. Every Thursday they dance with the village girls. So Thursday is a wonderful day for me! I can take a walk as far as the vineyards. But if the hunters danced at just any time, every day would be like every other day, and I should never have any vacation at all."

So the little prince tamed the fox. And when the hour of his departure drew near—

"Ah," said the fox, "I shall cry."

"It is your own fault," said the little prince. "I never wished you any sort of harm; but you wanted me to tame you..."

"Yes, that is so," said the fox.

"But now you are going to cry!" said the little prince.

"Yes, that is so," said the fox.

"Then it has done you no good at all!"

"It has done me good," said the fox, "because of the color of the wheat fields."

And then he added:

"Go and look again at the roses. You will understand now that yours is unique in all the world. Then come back to say goodbye to me, and I will make you a present of a secret."

The little prince went away, to look again at the roses.

"You are not at all like my rose," he said. "As yet you are nothing. No one has tamed you, and you have tamed no one. You are like my fox when I first knew him. He was only a fox like a hundred thousand other foxes. But I have made him my friend, and now he is unique in all the world."

And the roses were very much embarrassed.

"You are beautiful, but you are empty," he went on. "One could not die for you. To be sure, an ordinary passerby would think that my rose looked just like you—the rose that belongs to me. But in herself alone she is more important than all the hundreds of you other roses: because it is she that I have watered; because it is she that I have put under the glass globe; because it is she that I have sheltered behind the screen; because it is for her that I have killed the caterpillars (except the two or three that we saved to become butterflies); because it is she that I have listened to, when she grumbled, or boasted, or even sometimes when she said nothing.

Because she is my rose.

And he went back to meet the fox.

"Goodbye," he said.

"Goodbye," said the fox. "And now here is my secret, a very simple secret: It is only with the heart that one can see rightly; what is essential is invisible to the eye."

"What is essential is invisible to the eye," the little prince repeated, so that he would be sure to remember.

"It is the time you have wasted for your rose that makes your rose so important."

"It is the time I have wasted for my rose——" said the little prince, so that he would be sure to remember.

"Men have forgotten this truth," said the fox. "But you must not forget it. You become responsible, forever, for what you have tamed. You are responsible for your rose..."

"I am responsible for my rose," the little prince repeated, so that he would be sure to remember.

Chapter 22

"Good morning," said the little prince.

"Good morning," said the railway switchman.

"What do you do here?" the little prince asked.

"I sort out travelers, in bundles of a thousand," said the switchman. "I send off the trains that carry them; now to the right, now to the left."

And a brilliantly lighted express train shook the switchman's cabin as it rushed by with a roar like thunder.

"They are in a great hurry," said the little prince. "What are they looking for?"

"Not even the locomotive engineer knows that," said the switchman.

And a second brilliantly lighted express thundered by, in the opposite direction.

"Are they coming back already?" demanded the little prince.

"These are not the same ones," said the switchman. "It is

an exchange."

"Were they not satisfied where they were?" asked the little prince.

"No one is ever satisfied where he is," said the switchman.

And they heard the roaring thunder of a third brilliantly lighted express.

"Are they pursuing the first travelers?" demanded the little prince.

"They are pursuing nothing at all," said the switchman. "They are asleep in there, or if they are not asleep they are yawning. Only the children are flattening their noses against the windowpanes."

"Only the children know what they are looking for," said the little prince. "They waste their time over a rag doll and it becomes very important to them; and if anybody takes it away from them, they cry..."

"They are lucky," the switchman said.

Chapter 23

"Good morning," said the little prince.

"Good morning," said the merchant.

This was a merchant who sold pills that had been invented to quench thirst. You need only swallow one pill a week, and you would feel no need of anything to drink.

"Why are you selling those?" asked the little prince.

"Because they save a tremendous amount of time," said the merchant.

"Computations have been made by experts. With these pills, you save fifty-three minutes in every week."

"And what do I do with those fifty-three minutes?"

"Anything you like..."

"As for me," said the little prince to himself, "if I had fifty-three minutes to spend as I liked, I should walk at my leisure toward a spring of fresh water."

Chapter 24

It was now the eighth day since I had had my accident in the desert, and I had listened to the story of the merchant as I was drinking the last drop of my water supply.

"Ah," I said to the little prince, "these memories of yours are very charming; but I have not yet succeeded in repairing my plane; I have nothing more to drink; and I, too, should be very happy if I could walk at my leisure toward a spring of fresh water!"

"My friend the fox—" the little prince said to me.

"My dear little man, this is no longer a matter that has anything to do with the fox!"

"Why not?"

"Because I am about to die of thirst..."

He did not follow my reasoning, and he answered me:

"It is a good thing to have had a friend, even if one is about to die. I, for instance, am very glad to have had a fox as a friend..."

"He has no way of guessing the danger," I said to myself. "He has never been either hungry or thirsty. A little sunshine is all he needs..."

But he looked at me steadily, and replied to my thought:

"I am thirsty, too. Let us look for a well..."

I made a gesture of weariness. It is absurd to look for a well, at random, in the immensity of the desert. But nevertheless we started walking.

When we had trudged along for several hours, in silence, the darkness fell, and the stars began to come out. Thirst had made me a little feverish, and I looked at them as if I were in a dream. The little prince's last words came reeling back into my memory:

"Then you are thirsty, too?" I demanded.

But he did not reply to my question. He merely said to me:

"Water may also be good for the heart..."

I did not understand this answer, but I said nothing. I knew very well that it was impossible to cross-examine him.

He was tired. He sat down. I sat down beside him. And, after a little silence, he spoke again:

"The stars are beautiful, because of a flower that cannot be seen."

I replied, "Yes, that is so." And, without saying anything more, I looked across the ridges of sand that were stretched out before us in the moonlight.

"The desert is beautiful," the little prince added.

And that was true. I have always loved the desert. One sits down on a desert sand dune, sees nothing, hears nothing.

Yet through the silence something throbs, and gleams...

"What makes the desert beautiful," said the little prince, "is that somewhere it hides a well..."

I was astonished by a sudden understanding of that mysterious radiation of the sands. When I was a little boy I lived in an old house, and legend told us that a treasure was buried there. To be sure, no one had ever known how to find it; perhaps no one had ever even looked for it. But it cast an enchantment over that house. My home was hiding a secret in the depths of its heart...

"Yes," I said to the little prince. "The house, the stars, the desert—what gives them their beauty is something that is invisible!"

"I am glad," he said, "that you agree with my fox."

As the little prince dropped off to sleep, I took him in my arms and set out walking once more. I felt deeply moved, and stirred. It seemed to me that I was

carrying a very fragile treasure. It seemed to me, even, that there was nothing

more fragile on all Earth. In the moonlight I looked at his pale forehead, his closed

eyes, his locks of hair that trembled in the wind, and I said to myself: "What I see

here is nothing but a shell. What is most important is invisible..."

As his lips opened slightly with the suspicious of a half-

smile, I said to myself, again: "What moves me so deeply, about this little prince who is sleeping here, is his loyalty to a flower—the image of a rose that shines through his whole being like the flame of a lamp, even when he is asleep..." And I felt him to be more fragile still. I felt the need of protecting him, as if he himself were a flame that might be extinguished by a little puff of wind...

And, as I walked on so, I found the well, at daybreak.

Chapter 25

"Men," said the little prince, "set out on their way in express trains, but they do not know what they are looking for. Then they rush about, and get excited, and turn round and round..."

And he added:

"It is not worth the trouble..."

The well that we had come to was not like the wells of the Sahara. The wells of the Sahara are mere holes dug in the sand. This one was like a well in a village.

But there was no village here, and I thought I must be dreaming...

"It is strange," I said to the little prince. "Everything is ready for use: the pulley, the bucket, the rope..."

He laughed, touched the rope, and set the pulley to working. And the pulley moaned, like an old weathervane which the wind has long since forgotten.

"Do you hear?" said the little prince. "We have wakened the well, and it is singing..."

I did not want him to tire himself with the rope.

"Leave it to me," I said. "It is too heavy for you."

I hoisted the bucket slowly to the edge of the well and set it there—happy, tired as I was, over my achievement. The song of the pulley was still in my ears, and I could see the sunlight shimmer in the still trembling water.

"I am thirsty for this water," said the little prince. "Give me some of it to drink..."

And I understood what he had been looking for.

I raised the bucket to his lips. He drank, his eyes closed. It was as sweet as some special festival treat. This water was indeed a different thing from ordinary nourishment. Its sweetness was born of the walk under the stars, the song of the pulley, the effort of my arms. It was good for the heart, like a present. When I was a little boy, the lights of the Christmas tree, the music of the Midnight Mass, the tenderness of smiling faces, used to make up, so, the radiance of the gifts I received.

"The men where you live," said the little prince, "raise

five thousand roses in the same garden—and they do not find in it what they are looking for."

"They do not find it," I replied.

"And yet what they are looking for could be found in one single rose, or in a little water."

"Yes, that is true," I said.

And the little prince added:

"But the eyes are blind. One must look with the heart..."

I had drunk the water. I breathed easily. At sunrise the sand is the color of honey.

And that honey color was making me happy, too. What brought me, then, this sense of grief?

"You must keep your promise," said the little prince, softly, as he sat down beside me once more.

"What promise?"

"You know—a muzzle for my sheep... I am responsible for this flower..."

I took my rough drafts of drawings out of my pocket. The little prince looked them over, and laughed as he said:

"Your baobabs—they look a little like cabbages."

"Oh!"

I had been so proud of my baobabs!

"Your fox—his ears look a little like horns; and they are too long."

And he laughed again.

"You are not fair, little prince," I said. "I don't know how to draw anything except boa constrictors from the outside and boa constrictors from the inside."

"Oh, that will be all right," he said, "children understand."

So then I made a pencil sketch of a muzzle. And as I gave it to him my heart was torn.

"You have plans that I do not know about," I said.

But he did not answer me. He said to me, instead:

"You know—my descent to the earth... Tomorrow will be its anniversary."

Then, after a silence, he went on:

"I came down very near here."

And he flushed.

And once again, without understanding why, I had a queer sense of sorrow. One question, however, occurred to me:

"Then it was not by chance that on the morning when I first met you—a week ago—you were strolling along like that, all alone, a thousand miles from any inhabited region? You were on the your back to the place where you landed?"

The little prince flushed again.

And I added, with some hesitancy:

"Perhaps it was because of the anniversary?"

The little prince flushed once more. He never answered questions—but when one flushes does that not mean "Yes"?

"Ah," I said to him, "I am a little frightened—"

But he interrupted me.

"Now you must work. You must return to your engine. I will be waiting for you here. Come back tomorrow evening..."

But I was not reassured. I remembered the fox. One runs the risk of weeping a little, if one lets himself be tamed...

Chapter 26

Beside the well there was the ruin of an old stone wall. When I came back from my work, the next evening, I saw from some distance away my little price sitting on top of a wall, with his feet dangling. And I heard him say:

"Then you don't remember. This is not the exact spot."

Another voice must have answered him, for he replied to it:

"Yes, yes! It is the right day, but this is not the place."

I continued my walk toward the wall. At no time did I see or hear anyone. The little prince, however, replied once again:

"Exactly. You will see where my track begins, in the sand. You have nothing to do but wait for me there. I shall be there tonight."

I was only twenty metres from the wall, and I still saw nothing.

After a silence the little prince spoke again:

"You have good poison? You are sure that it will not make me suffer too long?"

I stopped in my tracks, my heart torn asunder; but still I did not understand.

"Now go away," said the little prince. "I want to get down

from the wall."

I dropped my eyes, then, to the foot of the wall⌐and I leaped into the air. There before me, facing the little prince, was one of those yellow snakes that take just thirty seconds to bring your life to an end. Even as I was digging into my pocked to get out my revolver I made a running step back. But, at the noise I made, the snake let himself flow easily across the sand like the dying spray of a fountain, and, in no apparent hurry, disappeared, with a light metallic sound, among the stones.

I reached the wall just in time to catch my little man in my arms; his face was white as snow.

"What does this mean?" I demanded. "Why are you talking with snakes?"

I had loosened the golden muffler that he always wore. I had moistened his temples, and had given him some water to drink. And now I did not dare ask him any more questions. He looked at me very gravely, and put his arms around my neck. I felt his heart beating like the heart of a dying bird, shot with someone's rifle...

"I am glad that you have found what was the matter with your engine," he said.

"Now you can go back home⌐"

"How do you know about that?"

I was just coming to tell him that my work had been successful, beyond anything that I had dared to hope.

He made no answer to my question, but he added:

"I, too, am going back home today..."

Then, sadly—

"It is much farther... it is much more difficult..."

I realised clearly that something extraordinary was happening. I was holding him close in my arms as if he were a little child; and yet it seemed to me that he was rushing headlong toward an abyss from which I could do nothing to restrain him...

His look was very serious, like some one lost far away.

"I have your sheep. And I have the sheep's box. And I have the muzzle..."

And he gave me a sad smile.

I waited a long time. I could see that he was reviving little by little.

"Dear little man," I said to him, "you are afraid..."

He was afraid, there was no doubt about that. But he laughed lightly.

"I shall be much more afraid this evening..."

Once again I felt myself frozen by the sense of something irreparable. And I knew that I could not bear the thought of never hearing that laughter any more. For me, it was like a spring of fresh water in the desert.

"Little man," I said, "I want to hear you laugh again."

But he said to me:

"Tonight, it will be a year... my star, then, can be found

right above the place where I came to the Earth, a year ago..."

"Little man," I said, "tell me that it is only a bad dream—this affair of the snake, and the meeting—place, and the star..."

But he did not answer my plea. He said to me, instead: "The thing that is important is the thing that is not seen..."

"Yes, I know..."

"It is just as it is with the flower. If you love a flower that lives on a star, it is sweet to look at the sky at night. All the stars are a-bloom with flowers..."

"Yes, I know..."

"It is just as it is with the water. Because of the pulley, and the rope, what you gave me to drink was like music. You remember—how good it was."

"Yes, I know..."

"And at night you will look up at the stars. Where I live everything is so small that I cannot show you where my star is to be found. It is better, like that. My star will just be one of the stars, for you. And so you will love to watch all the stars in the heavens... they will all be your friends. And, besides, I am going to make you a present..."

He laughed again.

"Ah, little prince, dear little prince! I love to hear that laughter!"

"That is my present. Just that. It will be as it was when we drank the water..."

"What are you trying to say?"

"All men have the stars," he answered, "but they are not the same things for different people. For some, who are travelers, the stars are guides. For others they are no more than little lights in the sky. For others, who are scholars, they are problems . For my businessman they were wealth. But all these stars are silent.

You—you alone—will have the stars as no one else has them—"

"What are you trying to say?"

"In one of the stars I shall be living. In one of them I shall be laughing. And so it will be as if all the stars were laughing, when you look at the sky at night... you—only you—will have stars that can laugh!"

And he laughed again.

"And when your sorrow is comforted (time soothes all sorrows) you will be content that you have known me. You will always be my friend. You will want to laugh with me. And you will sometimes open your window, so, for that pleasure... and your friends w ill be properly astonished to see you laughing as you look up at the sky! Then you will say to them, 'Yes, the stars always make me laugh!' And they will think you are crazy. It will be a very shabby trick that I shall have played on you..."

And he laughed again.

"It will be as if, in place of the stars, I had given you a

great number of little bells that knew how to laugh..."

And he laughed again. Then he quickly became serious:

"To n i g h t — y o u know... do not come," said the little prince.

"I shall not leave you," I said.

"I shall look as if I were suffering. I shall look a little as if I were

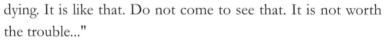

dying. It is like that. Do not come to see that. It is not worth the trouble..."

"I shall not leave you."

But he was worried.

"I tell you—it is also because of the snake. He must not bite you. Snakes—they are malicious creatures. This one might bite you just for fun..."

"I shall not leave you."

But a thought came to reassure him:

"It is true that they have no more poison for a second bite."

That night I did not see him set out on his way. He got away from me without making a sound. When I succeeded in catching up with him he was walking along with a quick and resolute step. He said to me merely:

"Ah! You are there..."

And he took me by the hand. But he was still worrying.

"It was wrong of you to come. You will suffer. I shall look as if I were dead; and that will not be true..."

I said nothing.

"You understand... it is too far. I cannot carry this body with me. It is too heavy."

I said nothing.

"But it will be like an old abandoned shell. There is nothing sad about old shells..."

I said nothing.

He was a little discouraged. But he made one more effort:

"You know, it will be very nice. I, too, shall look at the stars. All the stars will be wells with a rusty pulley. All the stars will pour out fresh water for me to drink..."

I said nothing.

"That will be so amusing! You will have five hundred million little bells, and I shall have five hundred million springs of fresh water..."

And he too said nothing more, becuase he was crying...

"Here it is. Let me go on by myself."

And he sat down, because he was afraid. Then he said, again:

"You know—my flower... I am responsible for her. And she is so weak! She is so naive! She has four thorns, of no use at all, to protect herself against all the world..."

I too sat down, because I was not able to stand up any longer.

"There now—that is all..."

He still hesitated a little; then he got up. He took one step. I could not move.

There was nothing but a flash of yellow close to his ankle. He remained motionless for an instant. He did not cry out. He fell as gently as a tree falls. There was not even any sound, because of the sand.

Chapter 27

And now six years have already gone by...

I have never yet told this story. The companions who met me on my return were well content to see me alive. I was sad, but I told them: "I am tired."

Now my sorrow is comforted a little. That is to say—not entirely. But I know that he did go back to his planet, because I did not find his body at daybreak. It was not such a heavy body... and at night I love to listen to the stars. It is like five hundred million little bells...

But there is one extraordinary thing... when I drew the muzzle for the little prince, I forgot to add the leather strap to it. He will never have been able to fasten it on his sheep. So now I keep wondering: what is happening on his planet? Perhaps the sheep has eaten the flower...

At one time I say to myself: "Surely not! The little prince shuts his flower under her glass globe every night, and he watches over his sheep very carefully..." Then I am happy. And there is sweetness in the laughter of all the stars.

But at another time I say to myself: "At some moment or other one is absent-minded, and that is enough! On some one evening he forgot the glass globe, or the sheep got out, without making any noise, in the night..." And then the little bells are changed to tears...

Here, then, is a great mystery. For you who also love the little prince, and for me, nothing in the universe can be the same if somewhere, we do not know where, a sheep that we never saw has⎯yes or no?⎯eaten a rose...

Look up at the sky. Ask yourselves: is it yes or no? Has the sheep eaten the flower? And you will see how everything changes...

And no grown-up will ever understand that this is a matter of so much importance!

This is, to me, the loveliest and saddest landscape in the world. It is the same as that on the preceding page, but I have drawn it again to impress it on your memory. It is here that the little prince appeared on Earth, and disappeared.

Look at it carefully so that you will be sure to recognise it in case you travel some day to the African desert. And, if you should come upon this spot, please do not hurry on. Wait for a time, exactly under the star. Then, if a little man appears who laughs, who has golden hair and who refuses to answer questions, you will know who he is. If this should happen, please comfort me. Send me word that he has come back.

The end.

作家生平解析

安東尼.聖修伯里
(Antoine de Saint-Exupéry)

法國著名飛行家、記者與作家。生於 1900 年 6 月，出身自法國里昂的貴族家庭。他以飛行員、軍人之姿的身分穿梭世界，以詩人的眼眸見證當時紛擾複雜的文明年代，使他的作品獨具一格。

聖修伯里四歲時便失去了父親，由母親一人扶養家中五個孩子。當中，聖修伯里和最小的弟弟法蘭索感情最好，但法蘭索卻不幸於 15 歲時患上風溼熱離世，聖修伯里在書中描述小王子離開地球時的文字，被視為法蘭索於無聲無息中逝去的樣貌：

一道黃色的閃光接近他的腳踝，
有一陣子他待在原地不動。沒有尖叫，
他像一顆枯樹般輕輕地倒下。
因為沙地的關係，他倒下時一點聲音也沒有。

聖修伯里自幼嚮往成為飛行員，但兩次報考軍校都未能如願。喜愛畫畫的他轉而報考建築藝術，只是短短 15 個月便自覺非志向所在而中途放棄。後來 1921 年受法國軍隊徵召服役，開始接受飛行員的培訓。退伍後，他轉入民間郵務公司擔任飛行員，往返西北非、南大西洋與南美各國。

　　1930 年至 1940 年間，聖修伯里為法國軍方效力，經歷 1935 年的一次嚴重意外，也不敵他再次重返航道，成為法軍的偵察飛行員。飛行的所見所聞提供他許多寫作靈感，《小王子》乙書就是描寫他於 1935 年墜落於撒哈拉沙漠的經驗，當時他正與他的副駕駛從法國巴黎飛往越南西貢，準備創下飛行紀錄獲得十五萬法朗的獎金。書中狐狸的靈感便是來自在撒哈拉沙漠中看見的夜行性生物 —— 耳廓狐，而其中一說也視狐狸為聖修伯里的知己里昂（前言中提到的大人）的原型。

　　聖修伯里多半著作都不在法國境內完成，就如同小王子利用候鳥逃離星球般，他的飛機也帶他離開自己的星球，航行於宇宙間。

　　1940 年法國被攻陷，他流亡於異鄉美國。而在此之前，他已出版的

《風沙星辰》在美國大獲成功，受到熱烈歡迎。但不諳英語的他，多次深感於孤島之中。反應出《小王子》中與蛇的對話：

「在人群裡也會感到寂寞的。」

他在美國足足待上了 28 個月，這段期間埋頭於寫作，妻子也從法國飛來與他團聚。起初居住在紐約中央公園旁的一間公寓，但因為過於吵雜不利於聖修伯里寫作，妻子便為他找到了一棟位於長島的貝文公館，其空間寬敞且華麗，共有 22 間房間。據說聖修伯里希望一邊就著陽光寫作、繪圖，會隨著光線一間一間地移動在屋裡的位置，就像小王子移動椅子，在一天之內看了 44 次日落般。

1942 年，在美國出版商與友人的建議下，他撰寫了童書《小王子》，然而他卻在前言中不忘強調，這是一本獻給大人看的童書。因為每個人的心中，都曾經住著一位小王子，聖修伯里的心中也永遠抽離不了小王子，他浪漫地書寫著，希望提醒每位大人「真正重要的東西是肉眼所看不見的」，不要忘記心中的那塊純真。

《小王子》於 1943 年在美國以英語、法語同步出版，獲得空前絕後的迴響。不過聖修伯里在出版幾星期後便重回二戰戰場，在 1944 年一次從科西嘉島起飛的間諜任務中消失，再也盼不到他的飛機降落，就如同小王子般靜悄悄地離開。而他沒能見證三個星期後法國解放，《小王子》也在那之後在法國出版。直到 2004 年，在法國馬賽外海發現了他當時駕駛的戰鬥機殘骸，從中找到了刻有他名字的手鍊，世人才終於知道了小王子的最終去落。

　*《小王子》初版中小王子在星球看日落的那天是 43 次，由於聖修伯里逝世於 44 歲，而後出版社便將次數改為 44 次。

小王子與玫瑰

　　眾所皆知，書中的小王子與玫瑰，便是聖修伯里描寫他與薩爾瓦多籍妻子 —— 康斯薇洛之間的關係。兩個人愛得濃烈，卻也因此互相折磨、難以相處，千絲萬縷的情感自始至終都無法圓滿。

　　書中任性、使小王子痛苦的玫瑰，沒能讓小王子留下，但小王子離開星球，即使在地球上遇見了玫瑰花海，也沒能忘懷生長於他星球上那朵獨一無二的玫瑰。有一說那玫瑰花海說明著聖修伯里的外遇，但他始終心繫掛念的永遠是他的妻子。

國家圖書館出版品預行編目資料

小王子 / 安東尼.聖修伯里(Antoine de Saint-Exupéry)作；
曾銘祥, 安東尼.聖修伯里(Antoine de Saint-Exupéry)繪；
姚文雀譯. -- 三版. -- 臺中市：晨星, 2020.09
　　面；　公分. --（愛藏本；105）
中英雙語典藏版
譯自：Le Petit Prince
ISBN 978-986-5529-46-8（精裝）

876.596　　　　　　　　　　　　109011609

愛藏本：105

小王子（中英雙語典藏版）
Le Petit Prince

作者｜安東尼‧聖修伯里（Antoine de Saint-Exupéry）
繪者｜曾銘祥、安東尼‧聖修伯里（Antoine de Saint-Exupéry）
譯者｜姚文雀

責任編輯｜呂曉婕
封面設計｜鐘文君
美術設計｜陳柔含
文字校潤｜呂曉婕

負責人｜陳銘民
發行所｜晨星出版有限公司
　　　　台中市 407 工業 30 路 1 號
　　　　TEL：04-23595820　FAX：04-23550581
　　　　http://star.morningstar.com.tw
　　　　行政院新聞局局版台業字第 2500 號
法律顧問｜陳思成律師

讀者專線｜TEL：02-23672044 / 04-2359-5819#212
　　　　　FAX：02-23635741 / 04-23595493
　　　　　E-mail：service@morningstar.com.tw
晨星網路書店｜www.morningstar.com.tw
郵政劃撥｜15060393　知己圖書股份有限公司
印刷｜上好印刷股份有限公司

初版日期｜2015 年 10 月 15 日
三版七刷｜2024 年 08 月 10 日
定價｜新台幣 250 元
ISBN 978-986-5529-46-8

填寫線上回函，立刻享有
晨星網路書店50元購書金